in the pines chris orlet

in the pines chris orlet

a small town noir

NEW PULP PRESS

Published by New Pulp Press, LLC, 926 Truman Avenue, Key West, Florida 33040, USA.

For information contact:
Publisher@NewPulpPress.com

ISBN-13: 978-1945734038 (New Pulp Press)
ISBN-10: 1945734035

Printed in the United States of America
Visit us on the web at www.newpulppress.com

For Trina

Black girl, black girl, don't lie to me
Where did you stay last night?
I stayed in the pines where the sun never shines
And shivered when the cold wind blows.

- Traditional

One

In the outer office of the Gideon police station, A.W. Stokes, a pasty, pear-shaped man with thin sandy hair and bloodshot eyes, was on the phone with the chief medical examiner. The M.E. was a Chicago fellow with a Polish name who spoke like he was in a big hurry and Stokes was only catching every second or third word he threw out.

"Say again?" Stokes said. "I didn't hear—"

"Arsenic trioxide," he repeated. "We found significant levels in her liver and kidneys."

"Arsenic?" said Stokes.

"White arsenic."

"I'll be damned." Stokes paused to wrap his mind around this new information. "How much you say?"

"A lot. A gram, at least. Maybe a bit less."

"Damn." Strokes pressed the receiver to his ear. "Yes sir, that sure sounds like a lot."

"That's because it is. Oh, and her stomach was empty, which isn't exactly surprising considering all the arsenic she ingested."

Stokes leaned heavily against one of the patrolmen's desks and stared out the front windows of the station. The windows were newly washed and the harsh morning sunlight flashed off the chrome bumper of a red '56 Chevy pickup and slammed Stokes square in the eyes. The chief squinted and turned away. The truck belonged to Fred Eggemeyer and the retired farmer parked it there every morning while he made his rounds: first to the diner, then to the barbershop and finally—if Jenna Hellebusch was in—the office of the *Greene County Herald-Tribune*. Fred had a serious crush on the *Herald's* sales manager. Everybody in town gave her grief about it.

Stokes picked up the phone and carried it to the window, cradling the receiver between his neck and shoulder, and dropped the blinds with a dusty crash.

"Chief Stokes?"

"I'm here," Stokes said. "It just don't figure. That girl weren't but sixteen. Good family...No sir. It don't figure at all."

"She was seventeen," the medical examiner corrected him. "I take it there wasn't a note?"

"Note?"

"Suicide note."

"Oh yeah. No, I don't believe so. It didn't come up. Anyway, her father would've mentioned it, I expect."

"Don't count on it."

"Yeah? Maybe you're right."

"I can tell you this much. She wasn't expecting."

That hadn't occurred to Stokes, that she might've been pregnant.

"No?"

"First thing we check. Well one of the first things. She was a virgin too. That ought to rule out quite a few things."

Stokes hadn't thought of any of that. But then he didn't get a lot of seventeen-year-old girls turning up dead. Save for the rare car accident victim.

"Her folks will be glad to hear that." Stokes said, and paused. "Well now 'glad' probably ain't the right word, is it?"

"Probably not."

Stokes shifted his weight from one sore foot to the other. He could feel Delores Campbell's eyes on him from across the room, awaiting the news.

"Anything else?" Stokes said.

On the other end Stokes heard papers shuffle and a

cigarette lighter click shut. "I think that's about it. I'll call the funeral home so they can come pick her up."

"That's fine," Stokes said. He started to put down the phone, but had another thought. "One more thing."

"Yeah?"

"How long's it take a young gal like that to die from arsenic?"

"How long?"

"Uh huh."

"That much arsenic trioxide, I'd say about two hour's sounds about right."

"Two hours."

"Maybe three, depending on what she had to eat."

"Yeah. Thanks again."

Stokes hung up the phone and stood thinking things over for a moment. Then he glanced at Mrs. Campbell who was staring at him intently. A puppy waiting for a treat. Stokes decided not to say anything. At least not right now.

He yawned and stretched his stiff back. "Suppose I'll go have me a little chat with Doc Summers."

"Doc Summers?" Mrs. Campbell said, her voice rising expectantly.

"Uh huh."

A phone rang. Mrs. Campbell ignored it. She followed the chief into his office.

Stokes went to his desk and picked up the keys to the cruiser and a pack of Lucky Strikes and his sunglasses. On second thought, he decided against taking the cruiser and tossed the keys back on his desk.

The phone continued to ring. Stokes lifted his eyes at Mrs. Campbell. "You going to get that?"

Mrs. Campbell frowned and picked up the chief's phone and punched the red button. "Gideon police. Delores speaking."

Stokes chuckled inwardly as he walked through the

front office and out the front door.

On the sidewalk he slipped on a pair of black Rayban Wayfarers and hiked west across Main Street. Stokes didn't often walk. Not more than a block or two anyway. Walking was for people who couldn't afford vehicles. Negroes and such. But it was a fine day. First day all week it hadn't rained.

He fired up a Lucky Strike and flung the match over his shoulder for luck. He strolled past Bob's Barber Shop and nodded through the open doorway to Bob Jennings who swayed back and forth in his one and only barber chair. Nearby sat Fred Eggemeyer in his standard faded blue bibs and frayed white cotton T-shirt. Fred had his hands folded over his ample belly. Both men nodded to the chief.

Stokes walked to the corner and waited as a line of trucks passed. Farmers, mostly. A few waved, most didn't. Stokes looked after one truck whose driver didn't wave and stepped off the curb and a horn wailed and Stokes started and jumped back up on the curb.

"Look out, sheriff!" the driver yelled.

Stokes frowned and looked both ways this time and started across the street. He turned the corner where Water Street curved uphill toward the bluffs, enough of a rise to make Stokes wish he'd taken the cruiser.

Doc and Ruby Summers lived in the old Wenzel place on a dead-end lane adjacent to a string of large, ornate nineteenth century houses. The homes were once the property of prosperous riverboat captains and were later purchased by coal mine and shoe factory owners, back when the proprietors of big businesses lived in the same towns as their employees. The gild and much of the paint had long ago worn away and most of the homes had been subdivided into three or four apartments. Some were owned by absentee landlords who allowed the homes to fall into disrepair, roofs and porches collapsing, cracked windows like jagged glass teeth, yards choked with chickweed and wild oats till the ruins all but vanished from sight.

The Wenzel house, by far the grandest home on the block, also served as Doc Summer's office, while Doc's wife Ruby doubled as his nurse, though she wasn't a licensed nurse. That didn't stop her from administering booster shots and taking temperatures and blood pressure and dispensing various medications. Stokes had been up to Doc's house a number of times, though always on business. Their relationship wasn't what anyone would call friendly, though it was civil enough. Doc was the physician of the over-sixty crowd, and Stokes was a mere forty-five. The younger generation preferred Dr. Fischer. It wasn't so much that Doc Summers was a quack — though lots of Gideon residents said as much behind his back — as he was out of touch. The practice of medicine had moved on since Doc studied at the state medical school in Springfield. There were new treatments and new theories of diseases Doc knew nothing about — despite being only ninety minutes from St. Louis. Stokes would see Dr. Fischer on those rare occasions he visited a doctor.

He was far from alone. When Dr. Fischer first set up practice it seemed like half of Doc Summers' patients opted to try out the new goods. To make up for the loss in clientele, Doc Summers began seeing colored patients, which caused him to lose another quarter of his clientele. No self-respecting white man was going to allow his wife or daughter to see a doctor who treated Negroes. After three months and a continued decline in patients, Doc Summers had no choice but to put an end to his colored trade. He still went on the occasional house call to a Negro home, but black folks were subtly discouraged from coming to his office.

Ruby answered the door in a crisp white uniform, her smile as stiff and starched as her outfit. Even the wrinkles around her eyes and jawline seemed to have had a recent run in with the iron.

"A.W."

"Ruby."

"You have an appointment?"

"No, no. This here's police business."

Ruby arched her eyebrows. "I see. Well, Doc's with a patient right now. He could be a while."

"That's fine," said Stokes, looking around the porch. "I'll just wait here on your porch swing and enjoy this fine spring weather."

"I'll see if I can't find you something to read."

"That'd be right kind of you."

"Can I get you some coffee while you wait?"

"No, no. I don't want you to go to no trouble."

"No trouble. I just made a pot not a half hour ago."

"Well in that case."

Ruby went inside and returned a moment later with a copy of the *Herald-Tribune*. Stokes had already read that issue, save for a few public notices and one story about a local invasion of stinkbugs, which he'd saved for the crapper. He sat on the porch swing and rocked back and forth till he grew slightly nauseous and read the insect story, suffering a mild sense of dread at the prospect of a stinkbug assault on his prize tomato plants. He turned to the county correspondent's section—a must-read for rural county natives like himself. There was a piece under Turkey Bluff News titled simply "Ordinances," which he'd somehow overlooked.

It is an ordinance within the village of Turkey Bluff that all premises and exterior property shall be maintained free from weeds or growth in excess of 10 inches. Noxious weeds are prohibited. Property must be free from any accumulation of rubbish or garbage. Disposal shall be done in a clean and sanitary manner by placing the rubbish in approved containers. It is also an ordinance of the village that no inoperative or unlicensed motor vehicles shall be parked, kept or stored on any premises unless it is in an enclosed garage, and no vehicle shall at any time be in a state of major disassembly, disrepair or in the process of being stripped or dismantled.

Rubbish *or* garbage? Stokes wondered what the difference was. He might have to look that up later. As for the inoperative motor vehicle ordinance, well, good luck enforcing that, Mr. County Code Enforcement Officer.

He scanned the top story again. The article was about the Ahrens girl, naturally. Biggest story in Greene County since the opera house burned down. When was that? Back in Forty-eight? The story contained a brief interview with the coroner. Roger Tully didn't have a great deal to say — unusual for him — only that there'd be an autopsy and that the Ahrens girl's body had been sent to the medical examiner's office at the capital. Stokes had a feeling that he didn't know any more about that girl's death than the newspaper readers. This wasn't strictly true. He knew about the arsenic. He knew most people figured she died of a ruptured appendix or something like that. That was the rumor anyway.

The screen door flapped and Stokes looked up from the paper. Ruby appeared beside him holding a white mug of coffee.

"I believe you take it black?"

Stokes got to his feet in easy stages.

"Kind of you," he said, meeting Ruby's eyes. Actually he liked his coffee with cream and sugar, but she couldn't be expected to remember that. He sipped the coffee. It tasted bitter and stale too.

"The doctor will be out directly."

The doctor. She couldn't say "my husband," or "Pete." Some people just had to put on airs.

Stokes nodded and thanked her. He set down the paper and sipped the bitter coffee and studied the large Victorian houses across the way. The home of Doc Toenjes, the town's one and only dentist, loomed directly across the street, but Doc Summers had the river view with its scenic vista of the Mississippi valley, the bridge, the wall of trees and pastureland beyond. That had to burn the dentist's ass.

Ruby nodded toward the newspaper. "So sad about that poor girl. Just tragic."

Stokes grunted sympathetically.

"Pete was just devastated by what happened."

Now it's Pete, Stokes thought.

"Course he did everything he could for her."

"Why sure," said Stokes. Still doing damage control for the old man. Probably worried about a lawsuit.

There was an uncomfortable silence. Stokes slurped his coffee and rocked uneasily on his feet. The sun slanted above the roofs of the Victorians and a spring breeze wafted across the porch and set off a collection of stained glass wind chimes. Stokes despised wind chimes, the way they ruined a perfectly peaceful atmosphere.

"He's just now finishing up with Mrs. Hofstader."

"That's fine."

The old girl must have sensed that Stokes wasn't going to reveal the reason of his visit so she excused herself and went back inside. Stokes pitched the rest of the coffee over the railing on a bed of begonias and marigolds and returned to the swing. He stared off into the distance, thinking about the Ahrens girl and what the chief medical examiner had told him. So much arsenic. Doc Summers might just crap his pants when he heard the news.

No sir, he wouldn't want to miss that.

Presently the screen door creaked opened and a frail, dried up woman in a flowery hat and a faded shawl shuffled out onto the porch. Ruby followed her out, one gabbing over the other. Stokes watched the old women hobble down the steps to the sidewalk and on toward a black Ford coupe, their talk uninterrupted.

Doc Summers ambled outside a moment later, cleaning his spectacles on his frayed lab coat. Probably the same coat he'd worn for the past 40 years.

"Morning A.W."

"Doc."

"Fine morning."

"Couldn't ask for a finer one."

Doc Summers breathed on the other lens and wiped the glass on his coat, then he held the spectacles up before his eyes and carefully studied his work. He seemed to approve and slid the glasses on his nose.

"Sorry you had to wait."

"No problem at all. Give me a chance to catch up on the Turkey Bluff news."

Doc Summers grinned. "Best part of the paper."

Stokes shoved his hands in his back pockets. "Got a minute, Doc?"

"Certainly. Let's go to my office."

Doc Summers led Stokes through a long old fashioned sitting room jammed with heavy wood furniture, threadbare rugs, thick dusty drapes, ghostly photographs and a few portraits of grim, long-dead ancestors to his study wedged into a back corner of the house. The room was cramped and windowless, the walls lined floor to ceiling with solid oak bookshelves groaning under a collection of battered leather books. The air was close and warm and smelled slightly mildewed. Dog-eared medical journals and yellow newspapers pocked with coffee mug stains littered an antique desk and a good deal of the carpet. Probably for show, Stokes thought. An ornery-looking tabby cat lifted its head from the worn seat of a tattered armchair and gave Stokes an icy look. The chair was thickly matted with orange hair and its arms and legs looked to have been partially shredded, doubtless by the same ill-tempered feline. Stokes hoped he wasn't expected to sit in the cat's chair.

Doc Summers shoved the cat off the armchair and motioned for the chief to sit.

Stokes looked around for another chair, but they were all piled high with leaning stacks of newspapers and magazines.

The doc was a goddamned packrat.

"Coffee?" Doc Summers said.

"Had some, thanks."

Stokes sunk down into the chair and removed his peaked cap and loosened his tie.

Doc Summers made a perfunctory attempt at straightening his desk, then he quickly gave that up and sat down. "How's the family?" he said.

"Oh fine. Everybody's fine," Stokes said without enthusiasm. "Your Ruby looks well."

"Oh sure. Fit as an old horse." Doc Summers slouched and gripped the arm of his swivel chair. "So what brings you by?"

Stokes cleared his throat. "Actually, I heard from the medical examiner this morning."

"Medical examiner, huh? I haven't talked to Les Payne in years."

Stokes shook his head. "This feller's name was

Sikorski."

"Sikorski? Don't know a Sikorski." Doc Summers thought it over some more and shook his head. "No sir, don't know a Sikorski. Sounds like a Polack. I wonder if Les retired."

"Couldn't say. Anyways, this feller called me this morning. About the Ahrens girl."

"The Ahrens girl," Doc repeated.

Stokes nodded. "Says she died of arsenic poisoning."

Doc Summers stiffened. "Arsenic?"

"Uh huh."

Stokes sat back and waited for the news to sink in.

Doc Summers swallowed hard, like he had a Ping-Pong ball lodged in his throat. His eyes searched the top of his desk.

"Arsenic trioxide?"

"I believe that's what he said."

Doc Summers chewed on a thumbnail. "Huh."

He moved around some folders on his desk till he found the one he wanted and he opened it and took out some papers. He studied one of the sheets.

Stokes tried to cross his legs, but his legs were too stiff and his trousers were too damn tight and wouldn't cooperate. He gave up and planted his feet on the floor.

At length Doc Summers looked up. "That was the official cause of death then? Arsenic poisoning?"

"That's what the man said."

The doctor shook his head. "It don't seem possible. It just don't seem possible."

Stokes held silent, enjoying himself immensely.

"I'll tell you one thing. That girl did not take arsenic knowingly. I'd stake my reputation on it."

What reputation? Stokes thought.

The doctor looked up. "Did he say if she was—"

"She wasn't pregnant."

Doc Summers nodded. "No. Of course not. Comes from a good family."

Stokes leaned forward and waited.

Doc Summers shook his head wearily. "No sir. That girl was not a suicide."

"How can you be sure?"

Doc Summers scowled. "I was there, wasn't I?" He paused. "That girl was scared. She had no idea what was happening to her."

"Sounds like nobody did."

Doc Summers flinched. He turned away briefly, stung by the remark.

Stokes brushed an imaginary piece of lint from his trouser leg, and smiled inwardly.

There was a rap on the door and Ruby poked her head inside. "Mrs. Hartlieb's here, doctor."

Back to doctor, Stokes thought.

"Thank you, Ruby."

Stokes studied the doctor. Despite himself, he was beginning to feel a little sorry for the old man. He'd probably have to spend the rest of his professional career defending himself, and his diagnosis, what he did and didn't do.

But how the hell could you miss arsenic poisoning?

Then again Stokes had no idea if arsenic was easy to spot or not. And it wasn't likely something a small town doctor came across everyday. In his fifteen years of police work he'd never seen it come up. Not once.

Doc Summers frowned for a moment, calculating. "This was not a girl who was suicidal."

"You knew her pretty well, then?"

"Of course. She was a patient."

"Mind if I ask when you saw her last? As a patient, I mean."

Doc Summers hesitated. He didn't like where this was

going. All these questions. He wasn't about to defend his actions to a layman, especially an uneducated boor like Stokes. Yes, she'd been a patient — till Dr. Fischer set up shop. Then she'd become a former patient. But Stokes didn't need to know all that. It wasn't relevant.

Doc Summers decided to cut things off now. This was no friendly chat over coffee. This was an interrogation.

Doc Summers glanced briefly at his pocket watch and stood up. He fumbled the papers back into the folder and stood up.

"I appreciate you coming by, A.W.," he said, extending his hand. "Now if you don't mind I have patients waiting. Hope you get to enjoy some of this fine spring weather. Lord knows I'll be cooped up inside all day."

Stokes tapped his fingers on the arm of the chair, then he stood up with a groan and took the doctor's hand.

"Good seeing you, Doc."

Doc Summers led Stokes through the sitting room to the front door. As he opened the front door, the doctor took hold of Stoke's arm and leaned in confidentially. "Do Walt and Marie know about this?"

"You're the first I told. I figured I'd ask them to come down to the station this morning so I can break the news to them. That is, unless you'd like to?"

The doctor nodded absently. "No, no, that's fine. I was just wondering."

Stokes sucked on a tooth. "Uh huh," he said. "Well then I'll be seeing you, Doc. Oh, and tell Ruby thanks for the coffee."

Stokes stepped onto the porch and set his peaked hat atop his head and slipped on his Ray-Bans. The spring air smelled fresh, like new mown hay and he took a greedy gulp of it.

"Old fart should've retired ten years ago," Stokes muttered.

He walked over to the swing, slipped the newspaper under his arm, then started off in the direction of the police station.

At least the walk home would be downhill.

Two

Walt Ahrens spent most of his first day back at work slumped at his desk staring vacantly at an arc of framed family photos, while numerous Styrofoam cups of coffee cooled before him. His business partner, Harvey Gilster, stayed busy on the lot and mostly left Walt to himself. Walt had told Harvey he couldn't take sitting around the house anymore, the endless stream of female sympathizers bearing weepy condolences and bean casseroles, and his wife, Marie, a veritable basket case. If only they could get on with the funeral, get some finality. But the state still had Emily up in Springfield, going over her inch by inch, inside and out, trying to figure out what the hell happened.

It was after ten thirty when Walt got up and walked out to the lot and leaned on the hood of a Pontiac. He smoked a Lucky Strike and stared off into the distance. Harvey watched him from the showroom window, convinced his partner had come back too soon. It was unseemly, the way Walt stood out there in the car lot like a shell-shocked soldier for the whole town to see.

Harvey was relieved when a young couple pulled onto the lot and Walt went over to greet them. Harvey kept an eye on them from the showroom window, while he talked to Jenna Hellebusch on the phone about their newspaper ad. From the looks of it the young couple were interested in the slightly used 1957 Dodge Coronet.

Walt pushed his fedora back on his head and rested his shoe on the bumper. He smiled feebly and commented on the fine weather. He asked the young couple their names and where they were from and a few other personal questions, but he didn't seem particularly interested in the answers. Presently, he turned his attention back to the

Coronet.

"Not a scratch on her," he said nodding toward the Dodge, which wasn't exactly true. The any one could see that.

"How many miles?" the young man said.

"Only twenty thousand. Owned by this old pig farmer from Steeleville. Drove her once a week into town for groceries and that's all."

"I don't want a car that smells of hogs," the young woman cried, in a tone both offended and annoyed. Walt saw that she wore her thin, mousey brown hair in a high ponytail tied with what looked like a white shoelace. The young man sported a military style crew cut not unlike his own.

"Did I say hogs? I meant to say dairy. Dairy farmer, I mean."

"Why'd he sell?" asked the young man.

"Didn't say. You know dairy farmers. They don't generally talk much."

The young couple exchanged a meaningful look. Walt judged they were still newlyweds. Married less than a year, anyway. This was likely their first big purchase as a couple. They might take some convincing.

The girl whispered something to the boy — Walt hated it when they did that — and the boy nodded. Then they both gazed off down the lot toward a row of sedans.

Walt thumped the hood. "Got a V8 with four-forty horsepower." He stepped to the back of the vehicle. "See these fins back here? Don't see fins like that every day, do you? And how about that chrome up front? More steel up there than a whole Chevy. Nice spacious car for a two-door. In case you're thinking about starting a family." Walt winked at the young man.

"I don't know," he said. "It's more than we planned to spend."

"How much did you plan—"

Harvey poked his head out the office door. "Walt, phone!"

Walt frowned. "Tell you what. I'll let you two talk it over." He opened the car door. "Here, climb in. Feel these seats. Check out the wall-to-wall deep pile carpeting. We can go for a test drive around the block when I get back, see how you like her."

Walt started across the lot. He figured it was Marie on the phone. She'd already called once that morning. Not about anything important, but just needing to talk.

He stepped into Harvey's office. "Who is it?"

Harvey shrugged and passed the phone to Walt.

"Walt," the voice said, "A.W. here."

Walt was slightly taken aback. "Yeah, A.W."

"I was wondering if you and the missus could come down to the station. Say, in a half hour to an hour?"

"Um. Sure. I don't see why not. What's going on?"

"I'd rather we talk in person. If you don't mind."

Walt felt his bowels tighten. His mind raced through the possible reasons for the call. "Okay. I'll swing by the house and pick up Marie and we'll be along directly."

Walt hung up the phone. Harvey glanced down at his desk like he was studying something important.

"I need to step away for an hour or two."

"Sure, Walt."

"There's some young people from Red Bud out there. Might be interested in the Coronet."

Harvey didn't bother to look up. "Go on. I'll take care of them."

"I'll be back after lunch."

"No need to hurry. Take your time."

Walt snatched his sport coat from the coat tree behind his desk and picked up the pack of Lucky Strikes and a chrome lighter from his desk and slipped them into his

17

coat pocket and hurried out the side door.

With his thoughts elsewhere, he didn't even notice the young couple staring angrily after him as he eased into the Buick and drove off the lot.

He pulled onto Route 3 and headed south toward town. He lit a Lucky Strike and cracked the window and turned on the radio. Ray Price was singing "Same Old Me." Walt drove a block and decided he couldn't think with the radio on and turned it off. A.W. must've got the autopsy results. That had to be the reason he wanted them to come in.

He turned onto his street and found his mother-in-law Anne's Pontiac parked in the driveway again. Walt cursed, but he was somewhat relieved there weren't any other cars. Marie's goddamn church lady friends hadn't given them a moment's privacy since Sunday morning. He pulled the Buick to the curb and stubbed out his cigarette in the full ashtray. Then he took a deep breath and eased out of the Buick.

An ugly black wreath hung above the front door where his mother in law had nailed it Sunday morning. She hadn't even asked. Walt strode up to the door and pulled down the wreath and carried it around to the back of the house. He lifted the lid of the tin trashcan and dropped it in. He crashed the lid down and walked back to the front of the house and gazed up at the spot where the wreath had been.

Better.

Marie and her mother were perched on the living room sofa like two blackbirds. Anne was speaking softly into the phone. Probably one of them damned church ladies. The heavy gold-colored drapes were drawn and the darkened room was crammed with wilting flowers. That was another thing Walt couldn't stand, another reason he'd returned to work so early: the overwhelming death smell of lilies, gladioli and other funeral flowers. The flowers had been stored at Harper's Mortuary, but when the funeral was postponed Joe Harper trucked them over to the Ahrens' house. They'd be dried up like an old well by time the funeral was held. *If* it was held.

Anne looked up and cut short her conversation and hung up the phone. Walt stood blinking in the archway, partially stunned by the odors. His wife turned slowly to look at him, her voice flat and tired.

"You're home."

"A.W. wants us to come down to the station."

Anne said, "Lord, what does he want?"

Walt ignored his mother in law. "Best get yourself ready." He turned and stepped into the kitchen. The place looked a mess. Emily's orange cat arched on the counter snacking from a casserole dish. The cat raised its head briefly from the dish and looked at Walt and smacked its lips. Walt went out the back door and sat down on the porch steps and waited.

He smoked another Lucky Strike while he waited, and looked out over the backyard past the chain link fence. His gazed drifted to the Parkers' backyard with its new sandbox and even newer swing set for the twins, then on past to the Harmon's, a riot of car parts and automobile junk littering a grassless yard. A Chevy pickup jacked up in the garage. Normally the sight annoyed the hell out of Walt, just thinking of its effect on his property values. But today he couldn't have cared less.

He felt someone hovering over him and his mother-in-law's voice drifted through the screen door. "She blames herself, you know."

It was eerie the way her voice sounded exactly like Marie's. Walt exhaled smoke through his nostrils and didn't say anything.

Anne opened the screen door a few inches. "They

quarreled the night before... before she died."

"Over what?"

"Nothing important. Clothes."

Walt looked away. "She needs time."

"I tried telling her—"

"She needs time," he said more forcefully.

Anne paused. "I was thinking I'd take her to see Doc Summers. Maybe he could give her something to help her sleep."

Walt felt his temper flare. "She isn't seeing Doc Summers. Nobody in this family's going anywhere near that goddamn quack." He dropped his cigarette butt on the step below him and ground it out with the toe of his shoe.

Anne fell silent a moment before she spoke again. "Well Dr. Fischer then. He might give her a little something. If you don't have time I could take her..."

Walt cursed under his breath and stood up and brushed past Anne. As he went through the kitchen and down the hallway he could hear Anne behind him shooing Emily's cat from the casserole dish. "I'll clean up a bit while you're gone," she called from the kitchen.

Marie stood at the front door staring into her purse like it was a deep well.

"Ready?" he said.

"I feel like I'm forgetting something."

Walt took her arm. "That's all right, we'll only be gone a little while. You don't need anything."

She stared blankly at her husband. "Where are we going?"

"I told you. To the police station. Talk with A.W."

"Oh yes."

He led her out to the Buick like he was accompanying an invalid. He could feel the invisible gaze of the neighbors on them, prying eyes poking through blinds, their inaudible whispers, "Those poor Ahrenses! What they must be going through!" He helped Marie into the Buick, then he turned the car around in the Parker's driveway and they drove west toward downtown.

The police station sat on the edge of Main Street where the business district ended and the Stauder farm began. The district stretched for nine blocks but had ceased abruptly at the corner of Fifth and Main when the Depression hit. After that business never really picked up again. The only buildings erected after 1930 were the new city hall, the new fire station and the new police station, one next to the other. At some point the town fathers decided if the good citizens of Gideon couldn't have new businesses or industry they would at least have new government buildings.

Walt parked the Buick next to Fred Eggemeyer's pickup. They sat in the car for a moment, then Walt said. "Marie, this is not your fault. None of it's your fault. You understand?"

Marie looked down at her hands holding her black purse. "If only I'd let her have those shoes..."

He squeezed her hand. "Marie, you've got to stop this. None of this is your fault."

Marie pressed her lips together and her eyes welled with tears.

She nodded silently.

He helped her out of the car and she leaned heavily on his arm. A buzzer sounded as they entered the station and Stokes came out of his office to greet them.

"Walt, Marie. Thanks for coming."

"A.W.," Walt said. He nodded to Mrs. Campbell who nodded curtly back.

"How are you, Marie?" Mrs. Campbell said, rising to her feet.

"Just fine," Marie said, hollowly. "How are you, dear?"

"Fine. I'm so sorry for your loss."

Marie nodded grimly.

The police chief led the Ahrenses to his office in the rear of the station and moved around some chairs for them to sit on and offered them coffee. He got no takers for the coffee. He sat behind his desk and ran his hand through what was left of his hair and anxiously tapped a pen on his desk.

He waited till the Ahrenses were situated, then he cleared his throat and said, "Well now, Walt, Marie, the reason I asked you down here is on account of I spoke to the chief medical examiner this morning."

Walt could feel Marie tense up. He took his wife's hand in his and applied pressure like one would to an open wound.

"I figured that's why," Walt said.

"I'm not sure how to tell you this other than to come right out and say it."

Walt nodded silently.

Stokes cleared his throat again and looked down at the desk briefly. "According to the state medical examiner your Emily died of poisoning."

Walt heard his wife gasp.

"Did you say poisoning?" Walt said.

Stokes nodded. "I know. I had the same thought. It don't seem possible."

"I don't understand," said Marie.

"Well—"

"What do you mean poisoning?" Walt said. "What kind of poisoning?"

Stokes paused. "The medical examiner says it was arsenic poisoning."

Walt sank back in his chair, unable to speak. He felt like he'd just had the wind knocked out of him. He looked briefly at Marie, but the expression of shock on her face made him look away.

"Arsenic?"

Stokes nodded, his lips locked tightly over his teeth.

"That's got to be some kind of mistake," Walt said.

"No sir. I don't believe so."

"You don't believe so?"

"There was no mistake, Walt. The chief medical examiner...I mean, it would be highly unusual for him to make a mistake..." Stoke's voice trailed off. After a moment, he looked up at the Ahrenses and said, "There'll be an investigation, no question."

Walt stared hard at the chief. "But the doctors, they were calling it the stomach flu or a ruptured appendix."

Stokes shrugged helplessly. "I know."

"How?" Walt said, his voice aching. "I mean, what did he say? The medical examiner. What did he say happened?"

"He don't know. They just find out the cause of death. They're doctors, Walt, not detectives."

"Well, where the hell are the detectives?"

Stokes paused to choose his words carefully. "Let me assure you, if there's evidence of a crime there will be an investigation."

"If?" Walt snapped. "Jesus Christ, you just said she was poisoned!"

The chief looked down at his desktop and drummed his fingers. At length he said, "I haven't spoken to Roger Tully yet, but I expect there'll be a coroner's inquest. And if they find evidence of a crime or suspect a crime was committed it will be investigated. I guarantee it."

Walt swallowed hard and glared at Stokes. Marie leaned toward her husband laid her hand on Walt's hand. Walt shook her off.

"I don't understand. Isn't the arsenic evidence of a crime? I mean, what the hell is it if it isn't evidence?"

"Look, I know you're going through a lot."

"Well ain't it?"

"It *could* be evidence of a crime. Or it could be evidence of an accident. Or even a..."

Stokes paused. "Something else."

Walt's face reddened and his eyes narrowed angrily. He started to his feet. "Are you trying to say my daughter poisoned herself? What kind of horseshit is this?"

Marie took hold of her husband's arm. "Walt, honey," she said.

Stokes held up his hands helplessly. "Sit down, Walt. I'm not saying nothing of the kind. That's why we need the coroner's inquest."

Walt sat down slowly. He let Marie hold onto his arm without brushing her away. "I don't understand any of this. You're the police. Why aren't you holding the inquest or whatever the hell it is?"

"It's the law, Walt."

"I'll tell you what it is," Walt fumed.

"Walter," Marie said.

"Don't Walter me."

A phone began ringing in the outer office. Stokes heard Mrs. Campbell pick up.

They sat in silence for a moment and Stokes tried to think of something to say, a way to wrap things up without sounding too abrupt, but nothing came to him. He hoped the call was an emergency and Mrs. Campbell would come in and interrupt them. Instead he heard her hang up the phone.

Walt looked up at the chief, his expression grave. "Somebody did this too her. And goddamn it, A.W., if you don't find out who did I will."

Stokes flattened his lips and nodded silently. Walt was upset. Too upset to be reasonable. Stokes didn't think there was anything else to talk about, so he pushed back his chair and stood up and came around the desk and put his hand on Walt's shoulder.

Walt stared down at the floor. Then he looked at the hand on his shoulder like it was a large cockroach. "Whoever done this is still out there," Walt said.

"Walt, we're going to get the bottom of this. Don't you worry." Stokes removed his hand and turned to Mrs. Ahrens. "Marie, I sure am sorry to burden you with this news."

Neither of the Ahrenses made a move to get up.

Stokes sighed and looked toward Mrs. Campbell. She was on the phone again and didn't notice his plea for help.

Walt said, "When do we get her back?"

"Hmmm?"

"Our daughter."

"Oh, I expect they'll send her back directly. I'd say Joe Harper's got somebody on the way to the capital now."

Walt stood up slowly and took Marie's arm and helped her to her feet. Stokes led them into the outer office. Mrs. Campbell hurriedly ended the phone call and stood looking on helplessly.

Walt turned to the chief. "When will this inquest be?"

"I'd have to ask Roger about that. Sometime next week, most likely." Stokes put his arm on Walt's shoulder again. "I'll let you know the minute we find out anything."

Walt took Marie by the arm again and led her outside where the late morning sun poured down like warm honey on the cracked sidewalk.

"Let's go home," he said.

Perhaps he wasn't ready to return to work after all.

Three

Services for Emily Ahrens were held Monday morning at the First Presbyterian Church on Tucker Street with the Rev. Jerome Sharp officiating. The preacher took as his text a reading from Paul's Letter to the Thessalonians:

Concerning times and seasons, brothers, you have no need for anything to be written to you. For you yourselves know very well the day of the Lord will come like a thief at night...God did not destine us for wrath, but to gain salvation through our Lord Jesus Christ, who died for us, so that whether we are awake or asleep we may live together with him...

Every pew was filled. Friends and the curious crowded into the back of church and strayed into the aisles. The *Herald-Tribune* would later report that more than two hundred people turned out for the services, including most of the high school student body who were given the day off classes. Doc and Ruby Summers attended the service, but arrived late, had to stand in the rear of church, and departed early. People seemed to shun them, and certainly no one got up from his pew to offer Ruby Summers his seat. News of the autopsy report had spread over the weekend, but the rumor that the Ahrens girl had died of a burst appendix that Doc Summers had misdiagnosed persisted. Even those who'd heard about the arsenic figured Doc Summers had somehow messed that up too.

"Time they put that old fart out to pasture before he kills someone else," Frank Hawser grumbled to his wife after services.

Emily Ahrens was laid to rest in Evergreen Cemetery, not far from the tomb of the state's first governor, H.

Shadroch Holmes, the *Herald-Tribune* reported. The newspaper often noted that the newly interred were laid to rest not far from the state's first governor. Gov. Holmes and Hal Keen, creator of the once popular 1920's comic strip Boxcar Frank, the King of the Hobos, were the town's only two celebrities, though the cartoonist's final resting place was out in southern California. Since he'd died impoverished on Skid Row no one was quite sure where he was buried. And no one, outside a few turkey-necked local historians and nostalgic comic book nerds, much cared.

Emily's marble headstone was adorned with a weeping angel and cost Walt one hundred dollars. The stone was inscribed:

Beloved Daughter
Emily Jane Ahrens
B. Feb. 12, 1941
D. May 4, 1959
Allured to brighter worlds and led the way

Walt and Marie decided to purchase the adjacent plots for themselves and for their fourteen-year-old son Jimmy. Though they wisely kept this information from Jimmy.

~ ~ ~

The coroner's inquest was held Tuesday morning in the basement of the county courthouse. Bob Norris, the editor of the *Herald-Tribune*, was first to show up. Unless the Red Army invaded West Germany in the next twenty-four hours the inquest was certain to be his lead story and the articles about the groundbreaking for the new natural gas project and the school board hiring a new freshman football coach would have to be squeezed in somewhere on page two below the fold.

Norris found the coroner in his office, a room so cozy it might've doubled as a broom closet. Roger Tully suppressed a frown when he looked up from his desk and found Norris hovering in the doorway.

"Basement conference room," Roger grumbled.

The editor stepped inside the office and helped himself to a chair. He crossed his legs and looked at Roger expectantly. It was a look that said, "All right, let's have it. You owe me." Norris's paper had endorsed Roger for coroner in the last election. Norris liked having people in his debt — especially people with inside information — even if they weren't completely sure how they'd gotten there.

He may have had inside information, but Roger Tully was a still an outsider in a town where they were few and far between. Truth was there was no reason for anyone to live in Gideon unless you'd been born there and couldn't figure a way out. Roger had come to town in '46. Originally from central California, he'd visited the town on leave with an Army buddy by the name of Walt Ahrens, and he'd fallen in love with the town. More specifically, he'd fallen for Walt's sister Diane. After the war, he took an apartment in Gideon. Eventually the romance with Diane petered out. She settled on a farmer from Steeleville, and Roger moved into an old dilapidated farmhouse outside of town. The locals were surprised and wondered who or what he was running from. Roger was surprised too. He'd meant to return to California, but then he got a job driving an ambulance, and volunteering for the fire department, and he decided he liked the people of Gideon, who were much friendlier than the people he remembered in his hometown. The feeling was mutual. People just naturally took to Roger, with his pleasant demeanor, his quick laughter, and the way he never said a negative thing about anyone. Twelve years after he moved to town they voted him coroner. Not that he had any competition. Now he had his eye on the county board chairman's seat and he looked like a shoe-in.

Especially with the *Herald-Tribune*'s endorsement.

Norris took out a scratch pad from his jacket pocket. The room had a sour smell to it, like rotten food. Rotten something. That was bachelors for you.

"Who's on the card?" Norris said.

Roger removed his reading glasses and sipped at a mug of lukewarm coffee. He took his time answering. "You mean who's testifying?"

Norris leaned in. "Yeah, who's testifying?"

"Well now..."

"Doc Summers?"

"Uh huh."

"Who else?"

"Lot's of people. Might go on all day."

"The chief medical examiner?"

Roger pulled up a sock. "Uh huh."

"Walt Ahrens?"

"Nope. Well, maybe."

Norris cocked an eyebrow. "Maybe?"

"Probably not. The wife is. Marie."

Norris nodded. "And?"

Roger glanced down at a sheet of paper on his desk and scowled. "A young man, friend of the deceased. The soda clerk at Miller Drug. The play teacher."

"Play teacher?"

"Drama teacher. Whatever you call it. Fellow named Jerome Todd."

"Oh yeah. I know him," Norris said. His brow furrowed. "Why him?"

Roger rose from his desk and picked up an armload of files and folders. "Because that's where the deceased was before she went to the drugstore. Now if you'll excuse me I've got a hearing to attend to."

Norris' chair was blocking the doorway. He stood up and moved the chair so Roger could get around him.

"Play practice, huh? At the high school?"

"Yes, at the high school."

"What play was it?"

Roger turned and looked at the editor. "What?"

"What play were they practicing?"

"What difference does that make?"

Norris shrugged. "Maybe none. But details are important to a story."

Roger shook his head and started down the hallway. "I don't know what the play was," he called over his shoulder. "You can ask the director. And close the door behind you, if you don't mind."

Norris snapped his scratch pad shut and closed the door to Roger's office and followed the coroner down the hallway and down the stairwell to the basement. Already three-dozen people slouched on benches or leaned against the walls in the corridor outside the conference room, some dozing, some staring at the floor or the space in front of them. Norris recognized many of them — fine, up-standing citizens for the most part.

Roger walked up to the Ahrenses who occupied half of a long wooden bench.

"Hey buddy," Roger said, putting his hand on Walt's shoulder and squeezing softly. Walt's eyes were full of red lines crisscrossing like a busy roadmap. A small piece of bloodstained toilet paper clung to the bottom of his chin where he must have nicked himself shaving. Roger turned to Marie and took both her hands in his. She wore a small black hat with thin veil and a crocheted dress. She seemed extremely frail, like she'd aged ten years since he'd seen her last.

"I'm sorry you have to be here," he said.

She flattened her lips and nodded silently. Roger patted Jimmy on the arm and quickly moved on. Norris nodded to a few people before sidling up to Fred

Eggemeyer who sat at the end of a bench.

"Surprised to see you here, Fred," Norris said.

"I was going to say the same about you."

"Ain't had one of these things in a while."

"Nope. Guess the last one was when that Hockmuth kid drowned."

"Sounds about right."

Norris left Fred and followed Roger into the conference room.

The florescent lights were still flickering to life when Norris entered the long gray room. Seven metal folding chairs surrounded a six-foot folding table for the six jurors and one alternate. Another folding chair and a small card table were set up in the center of the room for the coroner. Next to that sat a chair for the witness. The other half of the room was set-aside for the public. The coroner had no idea how many spectators to expect, but it appeared the janitor had counted on thirty or thirty-five.

Roger surveyed the room. "Going to need more chairs," he muttered.

Norris sat down in the coroner's chair. "Biggest story since the opera house fire, wouldn't you say?" he said.

Roger wasn't listening. He seemed to be going over something in his mind.

"Your first coroner's inquest, ain't it?" Norris said.

"Uh huh," Roger said absently.

"That's what I thought. I guess Horace held the last one, about five years ago when the Hockmuth kid drowned. God, was that five years ago, already?"

Roger didn't appear to hear.

"You weren't at that one, were you?"

Roger was counting chairs and didn't respond.

"Thirteen-year-old. Tried to swim into this underwater cave and didn't realize the river had risen and the cave was submerged. Drowned in there. Father swam in and fished him out. He almost drowned too. That one still gives me the willies thinking about it."

Roger turned toward the editor. "Not sure why you'd need a coroner's inquest for that. Seems pretty cut and dried to me."

Norris shrugged. "Well, I'm a fan of inquests. Only way a newspaperman ever gets to find out what's what. Can't count on the cops to tell you squat."

"Well, I'm glad we're of service to you."

Norris shook his head. Gee, what a grouch, he thought.

Roger turned and walked out into the hallway. "Are the jurors here?"

Four men and three women rose and followed Roger into the conference room. He glanced at the editor sitting in his seat. "You don't mind waiting outside, do you, Bob?"

"Hmmm? Oh sure."

When the last of the jurors were seated Roger stood and explained the process.

"This is not a legal proceeding," he said. "This is only to determine whether the manner of death was homicide, suicide, accidental or undetermined. You will hear testimony from six witnesses or so and then you will retire and deliberate. Any questions?"

A retired farmer cleared his throat and said, "I'm confused. Did you say this ain't legal?"

Roger scowled. "I said this isn't a legal proceeding, Mr. Felker. I didn't say it wasn't legal."

The man stared blankly. "So it's legal?"

"Yes. It's legal."

The man seemed only mildly contented with that answer.

"Any other questions?" Roger asked reluctantly.

A young man, in his early twenties, said, "How long will this take?"

"As long as it takes," Roger said.

The young man frowned and muttered something to himself.

Roger didn't ask if there were any more questions.

A door opened and the state's attorney, a young, brash fellow named Hopkins, slipped inside. Roger nodded to the lawyer and then he walked over and opened the doors to the conference room. Immediately the hallway emptied. Norris found a chair in the front row and took out his notepad and crossed his legs expectantly.

The thirty spectator seats filled rapidly and Roger had to go off in search of the janitor so he could fetch more chairs. This caused another ten-minute delay.

The inquest went on till noon and the jurors took another two hours to reach their decision. Afterwards Norris hurried back to his office, took the telephone off the hook and closed his door and started banging away on his old Remington.

The editor thought the article that ran in the next day's issue of the *Herald-Tribune* was the finest piece of writing he'd ever done. And it very well might have been.

Coroner's Jury Undecided in Teen-ager's Arsenic Death

A coroner's jury on Tuesday was unable to determine the manner of death in the case of a Gideon teen-ager. Emily Jane Ahrens, 17, died in the early morning of Saturday, May 4. The report of the chief medical examiner listed the cause of death as kidney failure due to arsenic poisoning. A coroner's jury was called Tuesday and charged with determining whether the death was natural, accidental, homicide, suicide or undetermined. After deliberating nearly two hours, the jury of four men and two women declared the manner of death was undetermined.

Coroner Roger Tully said that lacking any additional evidence the case was now dismissed.

Gideon Police Chief A.W. Stokes said the police department would not investigate the matter unless evidence of a crime came to light and thus far no evidence of criminal intent has been put forward.

The jury heard testimony from six witnesses, including the mother of the deceased, Mrs. Walter K. Ahrens; the attending physician, Dr. Peter J. Summers; a young friend of Miss Ahrens, Chief Medical Examiner Dennis R. Sikorski and Jerome W. Todd, Gideon High School drama teacher.

The first to testify was Mrs. Ahrens who told jurors that on Friday, May 3, the day before the teenager's death, Miss Ahrens arrived home from Gideon High School about three-thirty and appeared to be in good spirits. She and Mrs. Ahrens ate a light dinner of leftover meatloaf and salad, then, at approximately six-thirty, Miss Ahrens departed on foot for play practice at the public high school gymnasium.

The play was *Our Town* by Thorton Wilder.

Miss Ahrens returned home at approximately nine-thirty that evening. She told Mrs. Ahrens that after play practice she and her friends had stopped by Miller Drug for ice cream sodas. Miss Ahrens appeared to be in good spirits, her mother told jurors. Miss Ahrens joined her mother on the sitting room sofa for a few minutes and watched the television show *The Thin Man*. Around ten o'clock she began to get ready for bed. That was when she first complained about not feeling well and thought she might be experiencing menstrual cramping. Miss Ahrens went to lie down in bed and soon began feeling worse and commenced vomiting. At ten-thirty Mrs. Ahrens attempted to telephone Dr. Fischer, the family physician.

She was unable to reach Dr. Fischer, and telephoned Dr. Summers, who arrived at the Ahrens' home at eleven o'clock. Shortly after Dr. Summers arrived, Mr. Ahrens and his son came home from a Cardinals-Cubs baseball game in St. Louis.

According to Mrs. Ahrens, Dr. Summers examined the teen-ager. His examination ruled out menstrual cramps and appendicitis. He then questioned Miss Ahrens about what she had eaten that day. Mrs. Ahrens said she called the three friends who had been with Emily at Miller Drug and none reported feeling ill. Dr. Summers concluded the symptoms were likely the result of gastroenteritis and proscribed fluids and rest.

Mrs. Ahrens testified that Emily's abdominal pains worsened and that the teen-ager became very frightened. "She said, 'Mother, I'm so scared,'" a tearful Mrs. Ahrens recounted for the jury.

As Miss Ahrens' convulsions and severe abominable pain continued, the family grew more concerned. Dr. Summers telephoned St. Mary's Hospital in Hamilton and spoke with an emergency medicine specialist. The specialist also thought gastroenteritis was likely the cause of her distress and advised fluids and rest.

Around midnight Mr. Ahrens was able to contact Dr. Fischer who arrived fifteen minutes later. By then the teen-ager had slipped into a coma. According to the coroner's report, she died shortly after one o'clock in the morning.

One of the jurors asked Mrs. Ahrens if there were any arsenic in the home. Mrs. Ahrens replied that there had never been arsenic or any product containing arsenic in the home.

Jurors also heard from Ronald Taylor, 19, the soda clerk who served Miss Ahrens and her friends at Miller Drug. Mr. Taylor said he did not remember what he served

Miss Ahrens that night, only that there were four teen-agers at the back table and all ordered ice cream sodas. He said he probably served twenty ice cream sodas that evening, and to the best of his knowledge no one got sick from any of the refreshments he served. He said in the year and a half he has worked as a soda clerk he has never heard of anyone getting sick from any food or beverage served at Miller Drug.

The jury then heard from one of the teen-agers who accompanied Miss Ahrens to Miller Drug. He testified that he and Miss Ahrens and two friends, a male and female teen-ager, walked to the drugstore after play practice and each ordered an ice cream soda. He could not recall what kind of ice cream soda Miss Ahrens had, but said it may have been root beer with vanilla ice cream. He said that besides the ice cream sodas none of them ate or drank anything else while at the drugstore. He also stated that there was no food or drink available at the play practice, as far as he was aware. After finishing their sodas, he walked with Miss Ahrens part of the way home, leaving her at the corner of Elm and Baker streets. He said she was in a good spirits when he left her.

The fourth person to testify was Gideon High School drama teacher Jerome Todd. Mr. Todd testified that Miss Ahrens had attended play practice from 7 p.m. till approximately 9 p.m. though he saw very little of her as she was backstage working on sets. Mr. Todd testified that he could not be sure whether Miss Ahrens ate or drank anything while at play practice, though he did not notice any food or beverages backstage nor had he made any available. He said he spoke to Miss Ahrens only briefly toward the beginning of play practice and that she seemed like the "same old Emily." He did not talk to her directly again that evening.

Coroner Tully then asked Mr. Todd if the high school

theater arts program did not present the play "Arsenic and Old Lace" two years ago. Mr. Todd said they had, however Mr. Hoppe was drama teacher at that time. He said the play is considered quite popular with High School Theater groups. The play, written by Joseph Kesselring, concerns two elderly spinsters who poison lonely old bachelors with arsenic-laced wine. Mr. Todd said he did not know whether Miss Ahrens was involved in that production.

The jury then heard from Peter Summers, MD. Dr. Summers said Miss Ahrens' symptoms seemed to indicate gastroenteritis and Dr. Fischer did not disagree with his opinion. Dr. Summers said his diagnosis was also supported by St. Mary's Hospital emergency medical specialist, Ralph Kenny, MD., whom Dr. Summers telephoned shortly before midnight. Dr. Summers added that he had absolutely no reason to suspect arsenic poisoning. He said Miss Ahrens' symptoms, which included severe stomach pain, diarrhea, convulsions, and vomiting were for the most part similar to the symptoms of a number of maladies, including stomach flu. Dr. Summers stated that he had never seen a case of arsenic poisoning before Miss Ahrens' death. Asked why he had not sent Miss Ahrens to the hospital, Dr. Summers said he concluded the best thing for gastroenteritis was rest and fluids and that these could be had at home without upsetting the patient with a long car trip.

The final witness was chief medical examiner Dennis Sikorski, MD. Dr. Sikorski said he found elevated levels of arsenic in Miss Ahren's vital organs. More than a thousand times the normal level in her liver and the two hundred and thirty times the acceptable level in her kidneys. He said the cause of death was kidney failure due to arsenic poisoning. In response to a juror's question the chief medical examiner said "historically" when arsenic trioxide is used in a homicide the arsenic is administered gradually, not all at once. He said a large dose would seem to indicate suicide. A juror then asked Dr. Sikorski if he thought the large of amount of arsenic trioxide found in Miss Ahren's tissues indicated suicide. Dr. Sikorski said, "Not necessarily." The chief medical examiner refused to speculate on whether Miss Ahrens ingested the arsenic intentionally.

The medical examiner concluded his testimony by saying he hoped to discourage any "wild talk" about the deceased by saying that Miss Ahrens was not pregnant at the time of her death.

~ ~ ~

That week's issue of the *Herald-Tribune* sold out in a day. Norris thought that the last time that had happened was the VJ Day issue in 1945. "I could kick myself for not printing another five hundred copies," he told Fred Eggemeyer.

Four

Following the jury's decision Walt remained seated bolt upright in his folding chair, his hand clasped tightly onto his wife's hand, and peering around the conference room in a state of confusion.

"That's it?" he said.

He looked at the people getting up to leave and he stood up and started across the room.

"Walter? Where are you going?" Marie called after him.

Walt ignored her. He marched up to Roger Tully who was busy talking to the state's attorney.

Roger glanced at him and nodded. "Hey, Walt. Give us a second."

Walt turned and moved a few steps away. The men talked quieter now so they wouldn't be overheard. Walt stared at the floor, fuming.

At length the state's attorney shook Roger's hand and walked off. Walt seized Roger's arm.

"What the hell was that supposed to be?"

Roger pried off Walt's hand. "What was what supposed to be?"

"Why weren't there any lawyers or judges present?" Walt nodded in the direction of the state's attorney. "Why wasn't he asking the questions?"

Roger put his eyes on Walt, flat and hard. "Walt, why don't you take Marie and Jimmy home?"

"Don't treat me like a doddering old fool."

"Walt—"

"Undetermined? What the hell kind of ruling is that?"

Roger didn't know what to say to that.

"A goddamn waste of time is what that was."

Roger looked away, stung. He knew that when Walt got like this anything he said would only make matters worse. And yet he couldn't help himself.

"I know you want answers," Roger said. "We all do. But one thing I've learned since I took this job—"

Walt turned before Roger could finish his point and stormed away.

"Let's go," he snapped at Marie and Jimmy. Marie paused to look back at Roger, her expression apologetic.

"Marie!" Walt cried.

She turned and hurried after her husband.

~ ~ ~

He dropped Marie and Jimmy at home and waited anxiously till his wife was situated in her usual spot on the sofa and Marie's mother's car had pulled into the driveway, then he kissed Marie on the forehead and hurried out of the house. He drove straight to the police station, banged through the front doors and, without so much as a hello, asked Mrs. Campbell if the chief was in.

"He's on the phone," she said.

"I'll wait."

"Could be awhile."

"I said I'll wait."

Walt took one of the chairs along the front windows and sat holding his fedora in his hands and staring absently at the floor.

Goddamn chief of police couldn't even be bothered to attend the coroner's hearing.

The morning sun slanted through the open blinds. Beads of perspiration stood out on his forehead and seeped down his chest dampening his undershirt.

"Mind if I close these blinds?"

"Excuse me?" said Mrs. Campbell.

"The blinds. Mind if I close them?"

"Yes."

Walt frowned at her. "Yes, you mind, or yes I can close them?"

"Yes, I mind."

Walt glared at her. He thought about getting up and closing the blinds anyway, but figured it wasn't worth the trouble. He loosened his tie and unbuttoned the top button on his shirt and set his hat on the chair beside him.

Across town the bells of St. Michael's Church pealed softly and he wondered if there were a funeral this morning. He hadn't heard of anyone passing away— anyone else.

Presently his thoughts took a more spiritual turn. He'd never felt that he was particularly blessed or anything, but now he saw that he had been leading something of a charmed life: a fine family, a successful business, a good friend for a business partner, money in the bank. Beer and barbecue and baseball on the weekends. What more could you want? He'd been living the American Dream all this time and he hadn't even realized it.

A phone rang, snapping him out of his reverie. He cleared his throat and his eyes settled on the clock hanging above a gray filing cabinet. The wording on the face read, "Time to Change Fram Filters." He wondered vaguely if it was time to change his oil filter and decided he probably had another month. His eyes drifted about the room, settling on various signs and calendars and other junk. He could hear the chief in his office talking loudly to someone.

A young police officer entered through the back door. He sported a buzzcut just like Walt and black-framed glasses. The officer said hello to Mrs. Campbell and glanced briefly at Walt and punched his time card, then he waved to the chief and went back out the rear entrance.

Minutes passed. Walt clearly heard the chief hang up the phone. Mrs. Campbell, however, didn't seem to notice. Or if she had, she pretended not to. Walt waited what he considered a decent interval before he cleared his throat and said, "I think the chief's off the phone."

Mrs. Campbell didn't look up. Walt had a pretty good idea why he was getting the cold shoulder. She was probably still angry about the '52 Hudson he'd sold her boy Lenny. There was absolutely nothing wrong with that vehicle when it left the lot. And yet the old bitch had been telling everyone in town that he'd taken advantage of a returning war veteran.

That was hogwash, of course. She was slandering his good name and the good name of Ahrens and Gilster Auto Sales. Not only was there nothing wrong with the car, but the kid wasn't even a war veteran. Serving in South Korea didn't make you a war veteran unless you fought in the Korean War and Lenny most certainly did not. He was only ten years old during the war.

"But you can't blame her too much," Walt told Fred Eggemeyer, "what with a drunkard for a husband."

This too had got back to Mrs. Campbell.

After a moment, she rose and walked unhurriedly back to the chief's office. For a minute Walt lost sight of her, then he overheard some murmuring, and she reappeared.

"The chief will see you now."

Walt gave Mrs. Campbell a fake smile in passing.

Chief Stokes stood and came around his desk and shook Walt's hand warmly. "Walt, what brings you in?" he said. Stokes looked out the door and caught Mrs. Campbell pretending to be minding her own business and closed the door.

"Please, have a seat," Stokes said.

Walt pulled up a worn wooden chair and set his fedora on his lap. Behind him an oscillating fan that looked like it was manufactured in the forties noisily pushed warm air around the office.

"Had to be in court this morning or I'd have been at

the inquest," Stokes said. He looked down at his desk while saying it. "Hear the jury couldn't reach a decision."

Walt sat up and his voice tightened. "I don't even know what that was supposed to be. What the hell is a coroner's inquest, anyway? Waste of time, if you ask me."

"Well now—"

"Roger and me, we're like brothers. But he ain't a lawyer, let alone a judge. He's an ambulance driver, and a fireman, I guess. He's got no business running a courtroom like that."

"Well—"

"It wasn't in even a courtroom. It was in the goddamn basement. I guess the broom closet wasn't available."

"A coroner's jury ain't supposed to be a trial, Walt. It's only supposed to find the manner of death."

Walt paused. "So when's the trial?"

Stokes lowered his eyes and kneaded the muscles on the back of his neck. He waited a minute before answering. "Who is it you want to put on trial, Walt?"

"Hell, I don't know. That's your job, ain't it? To find out who killed my little girl?"

Stokes leaned forward in his chair, his arms resting atop the cluttered desk, his hands folded. He fixed his eyes on Walt, dead solemn. "Walt, we don't know that anybody killed Emily. The inquest didn't find—"

"I just told you that inquest was about as useful as a towel for a frog."

Stokes sighed. "Walt, we seem to be going around in circles, here."

Walt continued to glare at the chief, breathing heavily. "Are you telling me that's it? You ain't even going to investigate my girl's death?"

Stokes slumped back in his chair, his voice thick. "What would you like me to do, Walt?"

"I want you to find out who killed my daughter,

Dammit! I want to know why someone would poison my little girl!"

"We don't know that anyone killed your daughter, Walt."

"That's why you investigate it! Jesus, A.W. Do I have to tell you how to do your job?"

"I'd prefer you didn't."

Someone knocked on the door.

"Come in!" cried the chief.

Mrs. Campbell poked her head inside. "Excuse me, chief. I was supposed to remind you of your meeting with the mayor."

"Oh. Thank you, Delores."

Walt didn't turn around. He kept his eyes locked on the chief like he suspected something was up. A ruse, perhaps, to get him out of the office.

Mrs. Campbell looked at Walt and then turned back to the chief. "It starts in five minutes."

"Okay. Thank you."

Walt waited for Mrs. Campbell to close the door, then he lowered his voice, but just slightly. "Why don't you start with the people she was with that night? Why don't you talk to Miller? And those kids she was with at play practice? And that drama teacher? He's a slimy, beatnik sonofabitch, you ask me. And that boy that walked her home? Somebody needs to question him too. And not like Roger did. I mean, really question him."

"Like I told you before, Walt, there ain't no evidence of a crime being committed."

"Christ, A.W., she was poisoned!"

Stokes sighed and leaned forward, his elbows on his desk. "I'm going to be frank with you, Walt. I think homicide is the least likely scenario here."

Walt stared blankly at the chief, stunned. "You think Emily killed herself. That's why you don't want to investigate."

Stokes shook his head. "It ain't that I don't want to investigate—"

"My daughter had everything to live for. You'd know that if you'd been at the inquest."

"You just said you didn't trust the inquest. Frankly I'm confused, Walt."

"I'm talking about my wife's testimony."

"Okay."

The room fell silent.

Stokes leaned back in the chair and crossed his hands over his belly. The chair emitted a loud squeak. "Let me ask you something. Did you check Emily's room?"

"For what?

"For a note?"

"Note?"

Stokes nodded.

"There was no note."

"You're sure?"

"Goddamn it, there wasn't a note."

Stokes nodded. "What about a diary? Did Emily have a diary?"

Walt stared blankly at the chief. "A diary? How would I know?"

"Most teenage girls do."

Stokes stood up. "I have to go now. You want my advice? See if she had a diary or letters. If you don't want to read them, have someone you can trust. Your sister. Have Diane read them. Maybe they'll tell us something."

The chief snagged his cap from atop the coat rack and picked up his pack of cigarettes and lighter. He thought he might walk over to the county courthouse and see the coroner. See if Roger didn't have some idea how to handle Walt Ahrens.

"I'm real sorry about your daughter, Walt," Stokes

said. He held out his hand.

Walt looked at the chief. He wasn't going to do a goddamn thing.

Walt got up and turned and left the office without taking the chief's hand.

He walked right past Mrs. Campbell without uttering a word.

Evidently, he was on his own.

Five

Rachel Miller sat across the table from her husband holding a half-empty wine glass. She gazed absently out the dining room window, her head tilted, swaying slightly to the pulse of a Dave Brubeck tune. The record player was turned up loud. Far too loud for dinner music.

Her husband, Ben, stared into his plate of holishkes. Two cabbage rolls, no sauce, no sides. He could feel a headache coming on and the music was only making matters worse. He took a sip of wine and sawed into a cabbage roll and forked it into his mouth.

Cold.

He set down the knife and fork. His wife continued to gaze vacantly out the window, humming. She finished her wine and took up the bottle and poured herself another glass.

She hiccoughed and looked at Ben in a bemused manner.

"How's your dinner, hon?"

Ben looked at her, fighting off the urge to snap. She was obviously trying to pick a fight. The loud music, miserable dinner, too much wine. All the hallmarks of a looming quarrel, present and accounted for.

"Fine," he said, gritting his teeth.

"I'm so glad."

She turned back to the window, smiled drunkenly and said, "Isn't that cute?"

He followed her gaze to the window. A gray squirrel was drinking from the birdbath. A brown sparrow perched on the opposite side of the bath eyeing the squirrel warily.

Ben got up and turned down the music. Not all the way, but halfway. Hopefully not enough to set her off. He never knew what might set her off.

He sat down again at the table and thought things over. When had his wife become so goddamn unhappy? Rachel blamed her unhappiness on their move to the sticks, as she called it, but it wasn't that. She'd been unhappy when they lived in the suburbs, long before they moved to Gideon. From the time they got married.

It wasn't the sticks. It was him. Or so he thought.

Rachel hadn't made any friends in Gideon. Not that she'd tried very hard. A few women came over once during their second week in town, introduced themselves, invited Rachel to their church. How were they supposed to know she was Jewish? Her name was Miller, after all. There were lots of Millers in town. Christian Millers. Mostly spelled Mueller, though. When Rachel told them she was a Jew, things got awkward. Painfully so. Goddamn church ladies couldn't get out of the Miller home fast enough.

Her one attempt at becoming a genuine part of the community — running for the library board the summer after they moved to Gideon — was an unmitigated disaster. She'd gotten fewer than ten votes. After that Rachel didn't leave the house for a week. And only then to replenish her liquor supply, which was becoming more and more of a crutch for her.

"This is so fucking humiliating," she'd told Ben the morning after the election. "I don't know what I was thinking."

Ben winced at her coarse language. He was far more prudish than his wife. Even so, he tried to be sympathetic. "We're still new here. Still outsiders. It'll take a while."

"Yeah, maybe in another twenty years I could get another two or three votes, make it an even dozen," Rachel said. "To them we'll always be outsiders."

Now Ben's thoughts turned from his wife's unhappiness to his own source of angst, the drugstore, and how he was going to have to fire his one and only employee.

Rachel hiccoughed.

Ben looked at his wife, longing for a sympathetic ear. "I'm going to have to let Ronny go," he began.

Rachel turned to face him. "Who?"

"Ronny Taylor. The soda clerk."

Rachel sat up. "Has he been stealing from us?"

"No. Nothing like that."

"Then what?"

"We haven't had more than ten people at the fountain since that girl died. And most of them were out-of-towners."

Rachel glanced at him, her face confused. "I don't understand. What's that girl dying got to do with us?"

"Nothing. But you know how people are."

"I know how these people are."

Ben shrugged. "People talk." He stared down at the cabbage rolls, shriveled and dead looking, like severed fingers. "They're saying she might've been poisoned. Poisoned at our store."

A darkness filled Rachel's eyes. She started to rise from her chair. "Who? Who said that, Ben? We'll sue the lying sonsabitches!"

"How do I know who? Lots of people, from the sound of it. We're going to sue the whole town?"

Rachel sat down again, fuming. "I thought she killed herself? Didn't you tell me that?"

"I said she probably killed herself. People who take poison — young girls, I mean — it's usually a suicide. Statistically speaking."

Rachel scowled. She stared out the window again. The birdbath was empty now. The sun had slipped below the treeline and the rooftops washing the backyard in shadow.

"The people in this town, they're all Germans," she

said. "Dieterman. Ahrens. Voss. Heidorn ... Hasenpfeffer, or whatever. Of course they're going to blame the only Jew in town. They can't help it. It's in their goddamn anti-Semitic blood."

"It's not that," said Ben.

"The hell it isn't."

Rachel got up and walked over to the stereo console and picked up a pack of Pall Malls and shook a cigarette from the pack. She glanced around the room and went back to her seat at the table and lit the cigarette. She tossed her head back and jetted smoke toward the ceiling.

Ben hated it when she smoked during dinner. Not that this could be properly called dinner. He pushed the dish of cabbage rolls away.

Rachel stared briefly at her husband, then shrugged. She tapped the ash of her cigarette into Ben's dinner plate and stared absently at the painting above Ben's head. It was a rural landscape done in oil. Ben had inherited the painting from an uncle, or maybe it was a great uncle. The painting was vaguely impressionistic, or trying to be, and it looked like it might be of a couple of barns or red houses on a hillside and something that might have been a yellow factory. Rachel disliked the painting intensely, but her husband said it held sentimental value. Every ugly thing he brought into the marriage held sentimental value, which meant she couldn't throw it out like she would've liked to.

People must have thought she had no taste.

She was thinking about the people in St. Louis, not the philistines in Gideon.

Ben said, "I feel for him. The kid needed a break, so I tried to give him one."

Rachel shrugged. "So don't fire him."

Ben looked at his wife impatiently. "What else am I going to do? You tell me?"

"We could sell."

"Don't start."

Rachel drew on her cigarette and looked at the painting again and made a sour face.

"You think that kid poisoned her?" she said.

"Don't be ridiculous. What a thing to say."

"Then why fire him?"

"I just told you, we've lost ninety-five percent of our trade."

"So you take it out on an innocent kid?"

"So I should keep him on when we have no customers?"

Rachel said, "If you were half a man you'd find out who's spreading those lies and punch him in the goddamn mouth." After she said this she leaned back in her chair and studied Ben for his reaction.

Ben gave her one. He stood up and tossed his napkin on the table and stormed out of the dining room. He went down the hall to the bedroom and a moment later Rachel heard the front door slam. She took up her wine glass and drifted over to the front picture window and watched her husband climb into the Oldsmobile and roar off down Ninth Street.

Rachel sighed and turned from the window. Then she swayed over to the record player and turned up the volume.

Six

Roger Tully unzipped his jacket and draped it over the back of his chair. He loosened his tie and took a seat behind his desk across from the chief of police.

"Where you heading?" said Stokes.

"Rend Lake. Soon as I wrap up one or two things here."

Roger picked up a piece of string from his desk and looped it idly around a finger. "Supposed to have left Monday."

"I heard that," said Stokes. He removed his peaked hat and pushed absently around at the band. "Rend Lake, huh? Me and Misses got us a little houseboat down there."

"That a fact?" Roger said, without much interest.

"Thinking about taking a little time off in late May, maybe spend a week down there, before it gets crowded."

"Uh huh."

Stokes was always amazed at the compactness of the coroner's office. Not much bigger than a janitor's closet. No secretary either.

Well, that was the county for you.

Stokes studied the photographs on the bookshelf behind the coroner's desk. There was one that appeared to be the coroner shaking hands with the governor. Big deal. Stokes had shaken three governor's hands, and he had the framed photographs to prove it. Not that things like that mattered.

Another photograph appeared to show the coroner dressed like a hobo. Must've been when he was grand marshal of the parade.

The coroner made a real convincing hobo, Stokes thought.

Roger took up a stack of mail and studied the return addresses. A few of these he dropped straight into a wire wastebasket. "I'm guessing you're here about Emily Ahrens?" he said.

"Uh huh."

Roger nodded gravely. "Walt giving you a hard time?"

"Hell you can't hardly blame him. Something like that happened to my daughter I'd act crazy too."

Roger picked up a large yellow envelope and studied the address and set it aside. "Yeah." Roger shrugged. "Well, the jury had its say. I'd have voted the same way."

"So that's it, then?"

"Unless you know something I don't."

Stokes set his hat on his knee and slumped down in the chair. "Normally, a case like this, a teenager and poison, it's suicide. Case closed."

Roger nodded. "Usually."

"Course I didn't know her like you did. But from the sound of it she was a good kid. Better than average student. Involved in school, activities. Friends. Nothing to suggest otherwise."

Roger looked at the chief steadily. "I've known Emily since she was almost a baby. She was a good kid. No doubt about it."

Stokes thought this over. "Course we are talking about teenagers," he said, delicately. "They don't exactly behave logical, now do they? Especially girls."

Roger became silent.

"I ever tell you about this young gal I knew, back in Monroeville. This young fellow broke up with her, said some nasty things, and she went home and hung herself. Just like that. Nobody knew why she done it for the longest time. She didn't leave no note or nothing."

Roger didn't blink.

"A month or two later the boy tells one of his friends

and he tells somebody else. So on and so forth. It was a small town. Smaller than this one."

"Marie said she was in a great mood up till she took sick," Roger said, meeting the sheriff's eyes. "Course they say once you decide to kill yourself your mood improves. That's why these things are so often a surprise."

"Who says that?"

Roger waved his hand vaguely. "Psychiatrists...you know."

"Eggheads. Sounds like a bunch of horseshit to me."

Roger shrugged. He loved his adopted hometown but new ideas were not a Midwestern strong suit.

Stokes said, "Seems to me a young girl that was going to kill herself would leave a note. You know, to make the survivors feel like hell the rest of their lives. Apparently there was no note."

Roger shook his head. "That don't sound like Emily Ahrens at all."

"So what then, you think it was an accident?"

Roger unwound the piece of string from his finger. "How the hell would anyone accidentally consume that much arsenic? I'd say accident is least likely scenario."

"Well hell then, that only leaves one thing."

Roger looked past Stokes to the corridor where the old Negro cleaning woman pushed a mop down the hall. "Homicide? That's simply not possible."

Stokes stretched out his legs and sighed. "Yeah. We ain't had a murder here since the Thirties."

"Yeah?"

"Oh yeah. Hell of a thing, too. This old feller, Jack Muller, he got shit-canned at the shoe factory for being soused on the job. Come back the next day and plugged his boss with .38. Got off twelve rounds and didn't miss once. Had to stop to reload." A wry smile crossed his lips. "Yes sir, hell of a thing. Nobody raised a hand to stop him.

Guess they all hated the bastard's guts too."

Roger sucked a tooth and wondered vaguely if Paul's Bait and Tackle Shop was still open. He'd heard this story at least six times before, at least three times from Stokes. The last time he heard the story it was the shoe factory owner who'd been killed and he'd only been shot eight times.

"Now over in Sparta where they got them coloreds there's been two homicides. Two in the past ten years. Course they just kill their own kind, so it ain't no big loss." Stokes chuckled. "No sir, I sure wouldn't want that job. Imagine what would happen if one of them coloreds went after a white feller. Or God help us, a white woman. I wouldn't want to have to confront that lynch mob. No sir. Coal miners and niggers are a bad combination. No thank you."

Roger grunted. He'd decided not to participate verbally in the conversation any more. Otherwise the chief would never leave.

Stokes said, "Last time I heard about a young gal getting murdered was a few years ago over in Mount Vernon. Some drifter come through town raped and murdered a thirteen-year-old. I believe he was from Texas. Or California. Got the chair, if I recollect correctly." Stokes paused. "Guess what I'm trying to say is I don't see this being a murder case neither."

Stokes paused again.

"You wouldn't believe the rumors going around. I wouldn't even want to repeat some of them."

Roger waited for the chief to repeat some of them.

"Especially the ones about her father. I mean with you fellers being friends and all."

Roger leaned forward in his chair. His eyes narrowed like slits. "What are you saying, chief? Somebody saying Walt had something to do with Emily's death?"

"Hell, Rog, you know how people talk."

"That's horseshit," Roger fumed.

"Course it is. Hell, the girl was a virgin. Proven fact."

Roger stared hard at the police chief. "I'd like to punch whoever said that in the goddamn mouth."

"Why sure," Stokes said. "Who wouldn't?"

The chief enjoyed getting a rise out of people, but he usually knew when to rein it in.

Roger said, "I've known Walt Ahrens since we were eighteen. I know him better than most people in this town."

"Why sure. It's just people talking. People with nothing better to do."

"What the hell's wrong with people?"

Stokes shrugged. "Now that's a question for a philosopher, not a peace officer."

The men became silent a moment, then Roger gazed at his watch. He'd hoped to be on the road an hour ago. "So what do you do? Do you investigate?"

"I don't rightly know. Hell, I don't know what there is to investigate. This is the damnedest case I ever seen. I mean, case ain't even the right word. Sure it's a strange death, but where would you even start? Then again if I don't do something your friend ain't going to give me a minute's peace."

Roger nodded. He slipped the watch off his wrist and began winding the crown.

Stokes figured it was time to take the hint. He stood up creakily and shook his head. He had wanted the coroner's advice, but he wasn't about to go asking for it.

Roger looked up, relieved that the chief was finally on his feet. "Well good luck, whatever you decide to do," he said.

Stokes laughed. "Thanks." He turned to go, then halted at the door. "Oh, and pronounce a few dead for me."

"Huh?"

"The crappie."

The coroner laughed. "Yeah. I'll do that."

Seven

Jimmy dropped his Schwinn three-speed in the front yard and bounded up the front porch steps. Inside, his mother sat alone at the kitchen table, staring at something Jimmy couldn't see. The cupboard drawers were open and the countertop was a confusion of tin cans, jars and cartons.

His mother turned and got up and gave Jimmy a hug and kissed him on the head. The after-school hug was new.

"How was school?"

"All right."

"Do you have homework?"

"A little."

Jimmy set his books on the kitchen table and plopped down in a chair.

His mother looked away and wringed her hands. "Are you hungry? Would you like a little something to eat?"

Jimmy shrugged.

"How about a sandwich? We've got some nice deli ham from Schroeder's."

"Sure."

She went to the icebox and peered inside. The fridge was still crammed with casseroles and dishes from the week before, most of them untouched. Most of it would have to be thrown out. Nobody had felt much like eating in the past week, not even Jimmy who usually ate like a teen wolf.

She found some sliced ham wrapped in white deli paper and unwrapped it and studied the meat and set the package on the counter. Then she took out a head of lettuce.

"I don't need lettuce," Jimmy said.

His mother paused and put back the lettuce.

"Just ham and mustard please."

"How about some Swiss cheese?"

"Okay."

His mother moved things around in the icebox till she found the cheese, also wrapped in white deli paper, and the mustard, then she went over to the breadbox and took out of the Wonder Bread and began making the sandwich. She trimmed off the crust and cut the sandwich in half and laid it on a small dish and brought it over and set it on the table in front of Jimmy.

"How about a glass of milk?"

"Sure."

She selected a glass from the dish strainer and opened the icebox and took out the bottle of milk and filled the glass. Then she turned and froze. The glass of milk slipped from her hands and shattered at her feet, sending milk flying across the linoleum floor.

"Don't eat that!"

His mother snatched the sandwich out of Jimmy's hands just as he was about take his first bite.

Jimmy froze, wide-eyed and breathless.

She stared at the sandwich in her hands like she was holding something toxic. She went over to the cabinet beneath the sink and flung open the door and threw the sandwich into the trashcan. She stared into the trashcan a moment, then she turned and ran out the kitchen door into the back yard.

Jimmy sat at the table, his mouth hanging open, wondering what he'd done wrong.

After a moment he got up and crept over to the kitchen door and looked out the window. His mother stood in the backyard. He couldn't see her face, but he could tell she was trembling all over. He looked at the broken glass on the floor, the spilled milk, and wondered if he should clean it up. Then he turned back to the window. His mother had gone over to the little picnic table in the back yard and sat on the bench, hugging herself and rocking back and forth ever so slightly. She seemed to be staring at the ground.

Jimmy went over to the phone on the kitchen wall and dialed his father's work number. Harvey Gilster answered.

"Is my dad there?"

"Hey Jimmy. He's with a customer. Is it important?"

"Yeah."

"Okay. I'll tell him to call…" Harvey paused. "Is it an emergency?"

"Kind of."

"Okay. Let me get him. Hang on."

Jimmy waited. At length his father came to the phone. He sounded winded.

"What's up, Jim? You all right?"

"I guess so."

"You guess? Where's your mother?"

"She's out in the backyard."

"She all right?"

"I don't know."

"You don't know?"

Jimmy breathed in and held silent.

"Do I need to come home?"

"Uh huh."

"Okay," his father said. "I'll be there in five minutes."

"Okay," Jimmy said and hung up the phone. He walked back to kitchen window and looked out into the yard. His mother hadn't moved.

He went out on the front porch and sat on the steps. He decided he would wait there till his father got home.

Eight

Walt waited till Marie had taken a sedative and drifted off to sleep before he crept downstairs and went into the living room. The flowers were long gone, but the stench of the funeral parlor lingered. Jimmy lay on his stomach on the couch watching the ball game. The Cards were behind to the Giants, even though Bob Gibson was on the mound. Jimmy often raved about Gibson, how he was going to be the best hurler since Bob Feller. Maybe better. Walt stood next to the couch, arms folded across his chest, and watched the game.

"Still two nothing?"

"Uh huh."

Kenny Boyer was at bat for the Cards. Jimmy used to tease Emily about the crush she had on the Cards' third baseman. The mirror over her vanity table was like a shrine to Boyer. Baseball cards, autographs, clips from newspapers.

After a little while Walt said goodnight to Jimmy and turned and mounted the stairs, careful to walk on the sides of the steps where they didn't squeak so much so as not to wake Marie. At the top of the stairs he turned and walked down the hall and stopped before Emily's room.

Gary the cat waited in his usual spot outside Emily's door. The cat looked up at Walt and meowed plaintively. Walt hadn't been in Emily's room since Saturday afternoon when he'd gone in at Roger Tully's suggestion to look for some kind of note. Just to be one hundred percent certain, Roger said.

There was no note.

A week had passed and Gary the cat continued his vigil outside Emily's room. Sometimes Jimmy would take the cat into his room, but the damn thing wasn't interested in sleeping with him. He'd linger by Jimmy's door crying till he was let out, then he'd pad over to Emily's door and meow till Walt gave in and opened Emily's door for him.

The door creaked softly as Walt entered his daughter's room. Gary rushed past him and leapt onto the bed. Walt paused a moment on the threshold and listened for Marie, heard her soft snores, then slipped inside and closed the door behind him.

The room was stale and gloomy despite the white and red-fringed curtains, the white furniture and light blue walls. The bed was made up, just like always. Everything was in its usual place, as far as Walt could tell. On the dresser lay Emily's brushes and perfume bottles and whatnot in neat little rows. Her books were stacked on the little white table by the bed, their edges neatly aligned: *Madame Bovary, Wuthering Heights, Jane Eyre.* From across the room a company of stuffed animals gazed questioningly at him. Where would one even begin to look for a teenage girl's diary, assuming she even kept one?

Under the mattress seemed the most logical place. Walt got on his knees and lifted the mattress and peered underneath.

It was too dark. He couldn't see a damn thing.

He leaned over and switched on the lamp on the nightstand and reached under the mattress. Something lay sandwiched between the box spring and mattress.

He held it up to the light. A small pink book with the words *My Diary* inscribed in silver. The book had a small golden lock on it.

Walt stood up and tugged at the lock for a moment but the delicate little latch proved surprisingly resilient.

He got back down on his knees and lifted the mattress again and felt around for a key, but there was no sign of one.

Oh hell. The lock didn't look like much. Certainly not for a guy who'd taken apart whole carburetors. Walt slipped his pocketknife from his trouser pocket and sat down on the bed and went to work on the lock.

Gary the cat looked at Walt and yawned.

After five incredibly frustrating minutes Walt cursed and angrily ripped the cover off the book.

He opened the diary and peered down at the pages. He'd never really noticed his daughter's handwriting before. How girly and neat it was with curlicues and pretty little scrolls. The book was about half filled, with the first entry dated fifteen months earlier.

Walt felt his heart race. It was like looking at his daughter naked, but he forced himself to read on. He needn't read the whole thing, right? Just the last dozen or so pages.

Gary came over and rubbed against his arm. Walt shoved the cat away.

"Please God don't let me find anything awful in here," he muttered. "I don't think I could stand it."

He turned to a place about twenty pages from the last entry and began reading.

~ ~ ~

... during study hall T. asked if he could look in my math book. I have no idea why he wanted to look in my math book or why he would even ask me that. Everyone knows T. has a crush on E. Anyway I didn't let him. Who knows what he might have done?

Maybe it was rude of me. Maybe I should have let him. Most likely it would have been harmless. M.P. said no way should I have let him and I guess maybe she was right. M.P. usually is...

Who the hell were all these T's and E's and M's? Walt

wondered. Well M.P. was probably her friend Mary Pat. That much he could figure out. He turned to the next page and found some kind of list.

Ten Most Handsome Cardinal Players:
1. Kenny Boyer
2. Kenny Boyer
3. Kenny Boyer
4. Joe Cunningham
5. Gino Cimoli
6. Don Blasingame
7. Stan Musial
8. Alex Grammas
9. Larry Jackson
10. Bill White

Wow, she really was obsessed with Ken Boyer. The guy wasn't even that handsome. He looked like an auto mechanic. Probably a harmless infatuation, though. And what was with Bill White? His daughter had thought a Negro was handsome? Walt shook his head and flipped a few more pages at random and began reading. He was immediately taken aback by the first sentence.

~ ~ ~

God, I hate my mother. I was talking to her about going to M.P.'s party Saturday night and she had to remind me that I was grounded from going to any parties on account I got a C (a C+ mind you!) in chemistry. I can't believe anyone can be so cruel! Basically she is being a complete cow. I hate her. I know I don't really, though, even as I write this I know I still love her but I can't help how I feel.

To make matters worse she says I can't have new shoes because I still fit my old ones. I'm going to feel like a real germ if I wear the same shoes I wore last fall. New shoes don't even cost that much, and I really need them. She's only doing it because I get most things I want so she feels like she has to say no, so I don't get spoiled. God, I can't believe her. And now I've lost my keys and she'll have kittens if she finds out. Oh, I hate her and I hate myself for losing them. God I'm so angry. I know they're only keys but if I've lost them I'll go crazy. I hate losing things, but I do a lot. Oh I'm soooo angry...

~ ~ ~

Walt winced at the language. Those must've been the shoes Marie was talking about, blaming herself for. It was strange. Marie had never said a word to him about Emily hating her or about her losing her keys. Unless of course she had and he hadn't been listening.

Probably it was no big deal. Weren't daughters always angry at their mothers? Wasn't it a normal part of growing up? He remembered how his sister Diane had more than once told their mother she hated her. Once, when their mother had the flu or something and a hundred-and-three-degree temperature Diane told him that she hoped she died. Of course, she didn't really hope that. Now the two women were the best of friends. More or less.

Walt flipped ahead a few more pages. The entry was from a week before Emily's death.

~ ~ ~

Big News! Today J. asked me to prom! It was very sweet of him. We were at play practice and he asked me if anyone had asked me yet and I said no, not yet. I was starting to get worried no one would, especially with prom only a month away. How terribly humiliating that would have been especially with me being on the prom committee and everything. Almost

everyone has a date by now. At least everyone
who is going. I didn't tell J. any of this, of
course. I had no idea he was going to ask me! It
was a complete surprise! I don't think he was
even planning on going. I suppose he did it out
of pity, but even so, it was sweet of him.
Naturally I told him I would be happy to go
with him. What else could I do? It would have
been nice if a boy who really liked me had
asked me. I really did think R. might ask me,
but I found out yesterday that he asked L. Oh
well. J. and I will have fun and the main thing
is I have a date for prom...

~ ~ ~

Marie had told him that Emily was going to the prom
with the Hawser boy. That he remembered. Marie hadn't
sounded too excited about it. Sure the boy was a little light
in the loafers and his dad was a goddamn bully — had
been anyway — but Jackie seemed like a good kid. A kid
Walt would've trusted with his daughter anyway. And
there weren't many of those.

But who the hell was this R?

A cheer went up from the downstairs television. Walt
listened carefully and thought he heard Marie snore. Dr.
Fischer's pills seemed to be working, thank God.

He turned the page. There was something that looked
like a poem.

The gold brocade brought from Paris
shone hot with horsehair bows
should I linger in late winter
paved for a night of iron stone.

The blue shells that beget the rose
and took every gale in stride

a paucity of words and signs
for the ringing of distant bells

Walt scratched his head. He didn't understand a word
of it. What did Emily know about Paris? She'd never even
been to Paris, Illinois.

And those rhymes. Rose, signs. Stride, bells. They
weren't even close.

He turned the page and found the last diary entry.
According to the date, it was from two nights before her
death. He flipped ahead, making sure.

Nothing but blank pages. This was it. The last entry.

~ ~ ~

M.P. thinks I ought to take lifeguard lessons
at Perryville Y and try to get a job at the city pool
this summer. I told her I planned to babysit the
Harriman kids again this summer, but M.P. said
lifeguarding would be so much more fun and
profitable and we would literally get paid to tan! I
told her there was probably more to it than
tanning. Ha! I asked M.P. if the public pool didn't
hire mostly boys or older kids for lifeguards like
seniors or college kids home for summer break
and M.P. said that was true, but there weren't a
lot of kids with lifeguard certificates so as long as
we got certified we should be able to find a job at
one of the pools, maybe even the country club.
The more I thought about it the more the idea
appealed to me. I wonder how hard it would be to
get a lifeguard certificate. I'm a very good
swimmer so that shouldn't be a barrier. I am
actually starting to get excited about the idea!

I am definitely not excited about my
chemistry test tomorrow! Guess I better put down
my pen and pick up my chemistry book. Yuck!

~ ~ ~

That was it. The last entry. Just typical teenage girl stuff, as far as Walt could tell. Troubles with boys and mothers. No shocking surprises. But then what was he expecting? Back alley abortions? Trysts with her guidance counselor? We were talking about his sweet little Emily Jane. Walt flipped through the book again and came across a few pencil drawings, mostly of shoes and clothes.

He closed the book.

He picked up the torn cover and put the book back together and set it down on the nightstand and put the pieces of the lock and the pocketknife in his trouser pocket. Then he took up the diary again and replaced it under the mattress. Emily wouldn't have wanted Jimmy to see it. Or anyone else. Then he turned off the lamp.

The room was plunged into deep gray shadows.

Walt sighed and sat down on the bed and listened to the sounds of Marie snoring next door and the murmur of the baseball game downstairs. Gary lay stretched out comfortably beside him. Walt rubbed the cat between the ears. He purred softly.

It still hadn't hit him. It still hadn't sunk in. A week had passed and he was beginning to think it never would. That the grieving period had somehow slipped past him.

There is definitely something wrong with me, he thought.

Nine

Most evenings Ben Miller closed the pharmacy at seven o'clock, which also happened to be the busiest time for the soda fountain. If the fountain were real busy Ben would sometimes roll up his sleeves and wait on a few customers. He was even known to wash a few dishes from time to time.

Tonight the lone customer was a young cop named Joe Waddell, a dullard with an ass two sizes two big for the stool. Waddell leaned on the counter sucking a Royal Crown cola through a straw and drawing on a Marlboro and chatting with Ronny the soda clerk. The two men were second cousins. Not that that was unusual in Greene County.

Ben hung up his lab coat and locked the door to the pharmacy and pocketed the keys. He'd had three customers the whole day. The first, Mrs. Renfro, needed some Dristan for her sinus congestion, then two hours later Mrs. Gibbons stopped in for some Geritol for her tired blood, and finally, right at closing time Mrs. Frazier waddled in for a bottle of cough syrup. Ben couldn't ever remember having so few customers, not since he opened the store in the spring of 1955. Ronny showed up at five o'clock to open the soda fountain (the kid was surprisingly punctual) and Ben spent much of the next three hours avoiding eye contact and trying to work up the guts to fire him. And just when he felt he'd screwed up the courage, in walked Officer Waddell.

It was the policy of Miller Drug that cops drank free at the soda fountain — a holdover from the days when Don Schaefer owned the drugstore — and Waddell was the kind of deadbeat who could put away three, four sodas an evening. He was still on his first RC when he turned around on his stool and gave the store the once over.

"Kind of dead in here."

"Uh huh," said Ronny, examining the scuffs on his shoes.

"Why so slow?"

Ronny shrugged. "Mondays and Tuesdays can be kind of slow."

"But not this slow."

Ronny adjusted his paper hat and leaned against the back counter and shrugged.

Ben walked behind the counter and nodded to Waddell. There were no dirty glasses to wash. No ashtrays to empty.

"Kind of slow tonight," Waddell told the druggist.

Ben jammed his hands in his pockets and gazed around the store. "A little," he agreed.

Waddell looked at Ronny. "Boy that new Dog 'n' Suds was busy. I seen that on the way over."

Ronny picked at a scab on his arm and didn't say anything.

"Cars backed up a block waiting to get in."

Ronny yawned and kept working the scab.

"Haven't tried it yet myself, but I hear it's pretty good. Heard the root beer's supposed to be amazing," Waddell said.

Ronny removed the last of the scab, examined it, and flicked it away.

Ben shook his head, but held his tongue.

Waddell continued, "Might have to try it one of these days."

Ben snapped, "Well, nobody's stopping you."

Ronny and the cop both stared wide-eyed at the druggist, surprised by the outburst.

Ben flushed. "Sorry," he said, his voice trailing off. "It's this damned headache."

"I know where you can get something for that," the cop said, with a short laugh.

Walt faked a grin and opened the cash register. The bills were still wrapped in rubber bands.

The silence was broken by the piercing squeal of a vehicle burning rubber. All three men looked up, then Ben and Ronny looked at the cop. Waddell had his patrol car parked right in front of the store. He scowled and slid off the stool and hitched up his belt and tossed a two-bit tip on the counter. "Somebody's got a little too much juice in his jeans," he said. "I'll see you fellers later."

The police officer hurried out the front door and seconds later the blue and red lights on the cruiser bloomed and the siren screamed and the patrol car roared off in pursuit.

A moment passed. Ben looked over at the soda clerk and cleared his throat.

"Say Ronny, I need to talk to you."

"Sure."

"Let's have a seat."

Ronny followed his boss around the counter and they sat down on a pair of red-capped stools, leaving two seats between them. Ben cleared his throat again and reminded himself that in ten minutes this would all be over.

"So. Ronny. You've been with me how long now? About fourteen months, right?"

"Uh huh. Started March twentieth of last year."

Ben was impressed that Ronny remembered his start date. He'd had to look it up. He forced himself to look Ronny in the eye. The kid had a pronounced Adam's apple that bobbed up and down when he swallowed like a buoy in a turbulent sea. Ronny looked older than his nineteen years. The druggist thought how he didn't know a whole lot about him other than he and some other punks had stolen a car once and done time for it in the county detention center. And how shortly after he began working at the drugstore he'd bought a nice blue T-Bird, a used one, which he'd somehow manage to pay for on a part-time soda clerk's salary. And that for the past six months he'd been dating a little redheaded floozy named Brenda who liked to wear her plaid skirt hiked up above her knees, and was known for her furtive glances and bubble gum popping. She'd flirted with Ben on more than one occasion behind Ronny's back.

Or had it been his imagination?

Anyway, they must've broken up because Brenda never came around anymore.

Then again *nobody* came around anymore.

Could be there wasn't a whole lot more to know about the kid. Early on Ben had quizzed him on his plans, his goals, but he hadn't seemed to have any, at least none beyond working at the soda fountain.

What about college? Trade school? Ben had said.

Naw. School was for squares.

What about the shoe factory? An ambitious young man could make a decent living there. Even work his way up. Or what about the mines?

He wasn't interested. A lot of his friends had gone to work in the shoe factory and the mines, but Ronny wasn't having any of that. He preferred living rent-free with his grandmother in a ruined farmhouse on the edge of town, and the carefree, part-time job slinging ice cream sodas, listening to the jukebox and shooting the breeze with the customers. Back when there were customers.

You couldn't do a thing with a kid like that. In a way it made what Ben had to do easier. Maybe this would force Ronny to get his act together. Maybe Ben was doing him a favor.

He could tell himself that anyway.

Ben began again. "So I guess you know business has been bad lately. Real bad. Not just the fountain, but the pharmacy too."

Ronny got a confused look on his face, like he wasn't sure where this little exchange was headed. He swallowed hard again. Ben watched the Adam's apple bob up and down.

"The problem is...things just aren't picking up. In fact, they've gotten worse. Maybe they'll pick up again. Maybe they won't. But the way things are now, I just can't afford to keep the soda fountain open. It's costing me too much money."

Ben waited for the kid to say something. He honestly had no idea what to expect. A kid like Ronny, he might flip out and start smashing things, tell Ben to shove the crappy job up his ass, or he might grovel at Ben's feet, beg to keep his job or he'd lose his T-Bird.

A shadow crossed Ronny's face and his voice raised an octave. "Wait...You're firing me?"

"Like I said, Ronny, I can't afford to keep the fountain open—"

"But I haven't done anything wrong! I show up to work on time. I haven't stolen any money or anything."

"That's not why I have to—"

"Are you firing me because that chick died?"

"What?"

"That girl. The Ahrens girl."

"Of course not. That's got nothing to do with—"

"That's why people stopped coming in here."

"Well, I can't help that."

Ronny got to his feet. "It ain't me they're afraid of, you know."

"What?"

"People in this town, they know me."

Ben didn't say anything.

77

"You're the stranger here. You're the one with the arsenic."

"Arsenic? Who says that?"

Ronny shrugged. "Lots of people."

"We don't carry arsenic here."

"That ain't what I hear."

"Look around, do you see any arsenic?"

"Who knows what you got behind that counter."

"Oh for Pete's sake. People are really saying that? That I poisoned that girl?"

"Why else would they be staying away?"

Ben glared at Ronny. He wanted to seize the kid by the collar and shake him till his brains rattled. "Why would they be afraid of me? That's crazy. If anything, they should...you're the one with the police record. You think I don't know about you stealing that car?"

"I was just a kid then. I haven't stole nothing from you. Not a cent."

"Okay."

Ronny took a step back till he was safely out of reach. "People say you Jews been poisoning people for hundreds of years."

Ben's mouth dropped open. "What the hell's that mean?"

Ronny held silent.

"Where'd you hear that? Ronny?"

He'd rip him to shreds, the little shitass. "Everyone knows that girl committed suicide!" Ben shouted.

"Yeah?"

Goddammit, Rachel was right. They would always treat him differently. The first sign of trouble, they'd blame the Jew. Unbelievable.

Ronny took another step back, and grinned maliciously. "People around here ain't going to like this," Ronny said. "I was the only one sticking up for you too."

Ben clinched his fists. He wanted to strike the kid, a sharp slap across the mouth would have done both of them good.

Ronny turned and stalked behind the counter and picked up his jacket. Then he came around the counter and walked past Ben toward the door.

Ben watched him go. Then he remembered something. "The key!"

Ronny muttered something he didn't catch and slammed the door behind him, the bell tinkling merrily behind him.

Ben followed. He opened the door and called out: "I'm going to need that key."

Ronny stopped beside his T-Bird and took the key off his key chain. He held the key in his palm a moment, then tossed it down the stormwater drain.

"Go fetch it," he said.

Ten

Walt sat in his Buick out front of 21 Mill Street. A '59 Pontiac was parked in the driveway and Walt couldn't decide whether the car had come from his lot or Jim Murphy's lot over in Sparta. He couldn't recall Harvey saying anything about selling Frank Hawser a Pontiac and he knew for damn sure he hadn't. He never forgot a car sale.

Walt had gone to school with Hawser, been in the same class off and on for twelve years. Hawser had been a bullying sonofabitch then and he was a bullying sonofabitch now as far as Walt was concerned, even if he was president of the Chamber of Commerce.

What the hell kind of chamber president buys a car from across the county?

A shitbird, that's who. Wait till Harvey hears about this.

Walt shut off the engine and rolled up his window and gazed up at the house. A bent old man came down the sidewalk walking a black and tan dachshund. The dog squatted and crapped in Hawser's front yard. The old man looked around guiltily and he and the wiener dog hurried on. That stinking pile of shit on Hawser's perfectly manicured lawn made Walt feel a little better.

He'd spoken to June Hawser that afternoon on the phone. She hadn't sounded too pleased with his request to stop by. He'd been purposely vague about the reason for his visit.

"We don't need a new automobile, Walt," June had said.

"No, no. It's not that. I'd like to talk to your son Jack. Just for a few minutes."

"He doesn't need a car either."

"I'm not selling anything, June. I just wanted to ask him a few questions."

"You want to ask Jackie a few questions? About what?"

"Well, about Emily."

"Oh." June paused before replying. "I guess that would be all right. Jackie won't be home till after play practice though. Around eight." There was another brief pause. "I should really ask my husb—"

"That's fine," Walt said and hung up before she could say anything else.

Frank Hawser called Walt at the dealership later that afternoon, but Walt got Harvey to lie for him, and say he wasn't there. Harvey didn't have a problem telling people white lies. That was one of the qualities that made him such an effective car salesman.

It likewise made Walt somewhat mistrustful of his partner.

Walt eased out the Buick and walked up the sidewalk. The two-story Queen Anne with a wrap-around porch was fine. No doubt about it. Hawser was doing all right for himself. Of course he'd inherited his father's construction company. It wasn't hard to be prosperous if you had a thriving, established company dropped in your lap. It also doesn't hurt if you're a goddamn bully with a knack for browbeating city and county officials into giving you contracts.

Walt rapped on the door and waited.

Presently a little boy about five years old opened the door.

"May I help you?"

"Hi," Walt grinned. "You must be Stan. After Stan the Man, right?"

"Sam."

"Sam. Right. Your folks home?"

"Yes."

The boy looked at him blankly.

"Can I speak to them?"

"I'm not supposed to talk to strangers."

"Uh. Sure. Okay. Can I talk to your mommy or daddy then?"

The boy turned. "Mom! Dad! There's a stranger wants to speak to you."

The door slammed.

Walt heard low voices and rustlings and a moment later the door opened. Frank Hawser peered through the open door.

"Hello Walt. I tried to reach you this afternoon at the dealership."

"Yeah? Guess I didn't get the message."

"Tried several times."

Behind him, Hawser's wife cleared her throat and Hawser seemed to remember something. "Our condolences again," he said.

"Thanks." Walt nodded toward the driveway. "Nice Pontiac. New?"

"Yeah, thanks. So, June said you want to talk to Jackie."

Walt nodded. "If that's all right. Just a couple of quick questions. Won't take but a minute."

Hawser put his eyes on Walt flat and hard.

"What's this about, Walt?"

"Just a couple of questions. No big deal."

Hawser folded his arms across his chest, barring the doorway. "I got that. June said the questions concerned Emily. What kind of questions?"

Walt glanced behind Hawser and spied a gawky, pock-faced teenaged boy standing in the living room and wearing a worried look.

"Brief ones. Won't take but a minute." He grinned

flatly at Hawser. "Mind if I come in?"

Hawser scowled and reluctantly moved aside. "Come on in."

"Thanks."

They walked into the living room and Hawser motioned toward an armchair.

Walt nodded hello to June and Jackie.

"You've met Sam," Hawser said.

"Yes. We just met."

Hawser turned to Sam. "Why don't you go outside and play."

"I got homework."

"Then go upstairs and do your homework."

The boy stumped over to the staircase. He climbed a few steps till he was hidden from view and plopped down listening with his chin cupped in his hands.

The Hawsers took a seat across from Walt on a long faux leather couch, with Jackie between them.

Walt cleared his throat and looked at Hawser. "Would you mind if I spoke to Jackie alone?"

Hawser glared at him. "Yes, I would."

Walt nodded. "Okay." He leaned forward on his elbows. "So...Jackie...How are things?"

"Fine."

"Is it Jack or Jackie?"

"Jackie's fine."

"Okay."

Hawser cleared his throat. A small annoyance showed on his face.

"So, Jackie. The reason I'm here. Well, it's about Emily. You probably guessed that."

Jackie lowered his eyes.

"You and Em were friends, right?"

"I guess so."

"Well, you were going to take her to prom weren't

you?"

"Uh huh."

His mother turned to Jackie, somewhat taken aback. "You were?"

Jackie didn't say anything.

"Jackie, when were you going to tell us?"

"I was, but then—"

Walt spoke up. "Since you two were good friends I thought maybe you could help me understand what happened to Emily."

"Gee, Mr. Ahrens, I don't know. I mean, how would I know what happened?"

"Well, the night she died. Friday evening. You were with her at play practice and then at Miller Drug. Right?"

"Uh huh."

"And you walked her home."

"I didn't walk her home."

Walt lifted an eyebrow. "You didn't?"

"Not really. I walked home with her part of the way. But I left her at the corner."

"The corner?"

"Of Mill."

Walt nodded. "Okay. So you walked her home part of the way."

"We were both walking in the same direction. Part of the way."

"Okay." Walt shifted in his seat. "Is there anything you can tell me about Emily that night? Anything different about her? Anything you can think of?"

Hawser spoke up. "Nothing he didn't already tell the coroner's jury."

"I'd like to hear it from him, if you don't mind."

"Actually I do mind."

June reached across Jackie and rested her hand on Hawser's arm. "Frank," she said.

Hawser brushed her hand away.

They became silent and all of them looked at Walt. After a moment Hawser's look softened. "Aw heck, Walt, I'm sorry to be so brusque. I can't even begin to imagine what it must be like for you. I just don't like you dragging Jackie into this. He's told everything he knows. Why can't you leave the boy alone?"

Walt leaned forward, his shoulders slumped, and folded his hands before his mouth. He spoke directly to Jackie. "I'm really sorry if this makes you uncomfortable, Jackie. But there's just so much that doesn't make sense. There's so many missing pieces." He shook his head. "Don't you see, the only ones who can fill in those pieces are the ones who were with Em that night."

The room fell silent again. Jackie's mother clasped her hand over one of the boy's hands. He didn't try to remove it.

Jackie spoke up. "I'd like to help. I really would. But it's like I told Mr. Tully. We were at play practice. Em was backstage working on the sets. I was out front rehearsing. I hardly saw her. Then we walked to Miller Drug and had a soda and listened to the jukebox and talked about stuff and then we went home." Jackie shrugged. "That's it. That's everything."

Hawser stood up. "Satisfied?"

Walt ignored him. "And there wasn't anybody else who talked to her, or was maybe hanging around?"

"Not that I saw."

"When you left her at the corner, was there anyone around then?"

"I don't know. I wasn't really paying attention."

"And she wasn't troubled or scared or nervous or anything like that?"

"She was like always. Laughing. A little tired. We all were."

"Laughing?"

Jackie shrugged. "A little."

Walt turned that over. "Why didn't you walk her home the rest of the way?"

"Sir?"

"I'm just curious why you let her walk home alone?"

Hawser said, "Why wouldn't he?"

"I'd like to hear it from Jackie."

Jackie looked at his father, then back to Walt. "I—I don't know."

"You don't know?"

"No. I mean. I had a long walk ahead of me and it was late."

"It was late, but you let her walk home by herself."

June stood up. "I think that's enough," she said. "It's getting late. Jackie go on and finish your homework."

Walt said, "You were going to take Emily to the prom, right?"

"He already said that!" Hawser snapped.

"Why Emily?"

Jackie looked at Walt. "Why?"

"Yeah. Why her?"

"I don't know. She was nice, I guess."

Hawser stepped in front of Jackie. "Okay, Walt. You said a couple of brief questions. Now it's late." He turned to Jackie. "Go on to your room."

Jackie stood up and looked around the room uncertainly. Then he turned and walked slowly over to stairs and began climbing the steps. His brother got up and followed him.

Walt got up slowly from the chair and paused in the middle of the room, his hands at his sides, his voice choked. "I'm sorry, June. I didn't mean to upset you." He turned and moved toward the door.

Hawser fought to control his rage. "I don't want you

bothering our son any more, Walt. I mean it."

Walt opened the door. Then he hesitated in the doorway. "I'm sorry. It's just so hard..." His voice trailed off.

He closed the door behind him and stood outside on the porch. Dusk had settled in and the street was quiet save for the shouts of a few children playing hide and seek down the block and the humming of a streetlight. Across the way a television set glowed in a dark blue window. In the garage next door, a wrench clinked against concrete. Somewhere a mother called in her children.

Walt could not understand how the world could seem so normal.

Eleven

There were no stories about the death of the Ahrens girl in the *Herald-Tribune* that week. Readers scanned the columns for some new development and found only articles about the annual Hobo Days Picnic and Parade and the county budget and the high school athlete of the week. Nor were there any stories the next week.

Or ever again.

People who never set foot in the newspaper office save to renew their subscription or drop off a wedding announcement stopped by to ask Norris if there was anything new on the Ahrens girl, thinking the editor might know something too embarrassing or too delicate to print, but something he'd be willing to share with an old friend. Much as he hated to admit it, Norris didn't know any more about the case than they did.

Of course nobody believed it.

"So what the heck did happen? That poor little gal kill herself or not?" said Fred Eggemeyer, holding the newspaper before him and ruffling the pages.

"Don't know."

Fred lowered the paper and scowled. "Okay, so what do you *think* happened? Think maybe it was some kind of accident?"

"Can't say."

Fred rolled up the paper and successfully swatted a fly with it. "Can't say, or won't say?"

"Can't."

"Damn it, why can't you?"

"Because I don't know!"

Fred slouched in an old captain's desk chair and gazed vacantly out the front windows. Every time Fred stopped in Norris expected that old chair to splinter into a thousand pieces and he truly hoped he wasn't on the crapper when it happened.

"So for all we know it could've been a murder," said Fred. "Could be a murderer running loose in town."

Norris flicked the dead fly off his desk. "Unlikely," he said.

Fred was quiet for a moment, thinking. "Walt Ahrens sure seems to think she was. Murdered, I mean." He waited to see how the editor would take this bit of gossip.

"He doesn't know any more about what happened than you or me," said Norris.

"Ain't it you or I?"

"No, it isn't."

Fred shrugged. "Tell you what I think."

"I'm sure you will," Norris muttered to himself.

"I think she killed herself."

Norris lifted his eyes. "Because?"

"Easiest explanation. Easiest is usually right."

"Well, you do like easy."

Fred let that go. "Course Walt ain't having none of that."

"That's what I hear."

"Going around making people nervous with a lot of fool questions about his daughter. People are starting to avoid him. I can't say as I blame them."

Norris looked at Fred. He was a pain in the ass for the most part, but he sure knew what was going on in town and what people thought about it, and he didn't mind sharing what he knew. Hell, he positively insisted on sharing. Norris just had to be careful what he said around him because an hour later it'd be all over town.

"That can't be good for the car business," Norris said.

"I expect Harv will have a talk with him soon enough. Course they can't be doing near as bad as the drugstore.

That place has turned into a ghost town. People are afraid to go within five hundred feet of there. Afraid they'll end up being served an arsenic soda."

Norris shook his head but kept silent. He didn't want to encourage that kind of irresponsible talk.

Fred yawned and scratched at a tick bite behind his ear. "You hear Miller fired that Taylor boy?"

Norris cocked an eyebrow. "Ronny Taylor?"

Fred nodded smugly.

"Beats me why he ever hired him."

"You know these do-gooders. Always trying to help a black sheep."

Norris nodded. "Why'd he fire him?"

"That's what a lot of folks are asking. Suppose he thought firing him would bring some trade back." Fred chuckled. "He was sure wrong about that. That only turned the rest of the town against him. Those that weren't already taking their business elsewhere." Fred paused. "This whole thing's been a boon for Ron."

"Who?"

"Ron Trost. Ron's Pharmacy over in Sparta."

"Oh."

"Yes sir. Miller may as well start packing and go back to St. Louis or wherever the heck he come from."

"Now Fred."

"Just saying what everybody's thinking."

"Uh huh."

Fred lifted his feed cap and wiped sweat from his brow. Then he rested his arms on his ample belly. "Still, ain't it the damnedest thing, that coroner's jury? What'd they say it was? Undecided?"

"Undetermined."

"Is that what they said? I thought they said—"

"I don't know. Unexplained deaths happen all the time."

"Not around here," Fred said. "You ask me, I think it was a suicide."

"Yeah, you said that."

"Nothing else makes any sense."

"I don't know. Doc Summers and Doc Fischer both said they didn't think it was suicide."

"Doc Fischer said that?"

Norris paused before replying. "Well, off the record."

Fred nodded. "I was going to say. He didn't testify at that coroner inquest."

"No. He told me off the record." Norris laughed. "Damn. And I just told you. That's like printing it in bold seventy-two-point type on the front page. All caps."

Fred chuckled, then gave the editor a double-take, like he wasn't quite sure if he'd just been insulted.

Norris said, "I remember a story ran in the DuQuoin paper about this family got sick when one of the kids went out to the granary one night and mistook some arsenic for flour and it ended up in the noodles."

"That sounds like an old wives' tale to me," said Fred. "What the heck's arsenic taste like anyway?"

"I don't think it tastes like anything," Norris said. "Why they called it the inheritor's powder."

"Who did?"

Norris waved a hand. "People. Historically."

"Oh, him."

Norris reached into a drawer and pulled out his pipe and a tin of Captain Black. He stuffed the pipe with tobacco and struck a stick match on the wall behind him. Norris favored cob pipes on account of his two heroes, Henry Mencken and Gen. Douglas McArthur, both smoked them. Also, he liked to be different in small, innocuous ways.

Norris put his wingtips up on the desk and sent a cloud of smoke streaming toward the ceiling.

The front door opened and a middle-aged woman stepped inside. Norris frowned and removed his shoes from the desk. The woman glanced briefly at Fred then turned her attention to the editor.

"Mr. Norris, we didn't get our *Herald-Tribune* today."

"No?"

"So I thought I'd come by to pick one up seeing as I was downtown. I wanted to see if there was anything new on that poor Ahrens girl." She looked at Fred again and said hello.

"Hello Wanda. How's Al?"

"Mean as a snake since he lost the toes on his right foot."

"Reckon I'd be mean too."

"Can't stand without a cane. Pitches right over." Wanda turned to Norris. "How come the paper's been so late this past month?"

Norris shrugged. "Shouldn't be. I'll have a talk with your paperboy."

"Ain't nothing knew on the Ahrens girl, Wanda," Fred said. "I already looked."

"No?" Wanda said. "Why in heavens not?"

"Bob here says it's cased closed. Says there's nothing more to say."

"I can speak for myself," Norris snapped.

"Ain't the police going to investigate?"

Norris sighed. "If you'd read last week's paper—"

"I always read the paper. Except for the sports section. I don't have much interest in the sports section."

"Yes, well in last week's paper the chief was quoted as saying he won't investigate unless there's evidence of a crime. And no evidence of a crime has turned up." He held Wanda's gaze. "You don't know of any such evidence do you, Wanda?"

Wanda gave the editor a sour look. "Why would I

know anything?"

Norris shrugged. "Then I guess there's nothing left to say."

Mrs. Hatch set the newspaper down. "Please have a word with that paperboy, Mr. Norris."

"You can count on it," Norris said.

After the door closed, Fred winked and said, "I used to date her sister. Marsha Hollerbeck. She married Jim Brewer?"

Norris puffed his cob pipe and nodded.

"Jim's been dead, hell, almost twenty years now."

Fred tended to work into nearly every conversation how long somebody's been dead.

"Twenty years? Mourning period's over. What're you waiting for?"

"Ha!" Fred laughed. "I've gone sixty-eight years without getting tied down. Ain't about to end my winning streak this late in the game."

"I suppose not," Norris said.

Fred wasn't too bad for an old gossip. You just had to be careful what you said around him or it'd come back to bite you in the ass. Like that off-the-record remark by Doc Fischer. By tomorrow morning it would be common knowledge and Doc would be hotter than a July firecracker.

Norris figured he'd give Fred another five minutes of his time, then he'd get back to work, back to digging through the mail and writing up obituaries and sports scores. After five minutes of monosyllables Fred usually took the hint and moved on to his next stop, the barbershop.

Fred stretched and yawned loudly. After a while he said, "Jenna coming in today?"

"She was in this morning. Just missed her."

Fred stood up with a long groan. "Well, I got those

tomatoes I promised her out in the truck. Maybe I'll stop by later, see if she's in."

He shuffled toward the door.

"You could leave them with me," said Norris. "I'll see she gets them."

Fred said, "I don't mind stopping by later."

No, you don't, thought Norris.

Twelve

Jimmy lay on the couch staring vacantly at the flickering screen. Once again the Cards were getting hammered by the Pirates. He thought about turning off the set and going upstairs to finish his homework.

That's how bad it was.

Homework, however, was algebra, and that was even more painful than watching St. Louis down by four runs in the bottom of the seventh. Besides the Cards could still turn things around. And Musial was at the plate. Sure he was coming off his worst season ever, a measly .255 batting average. Sure he was thirty-nine years old and people were starting to grouse, making cracks about the retirement home, but he was still Stan the Man. Weren't nobody better.

Sometimes, laying there on the couch, lost in the action, Jimmy would start to say something to the empty armchair were Emily used to curl up watching the ball game. Then it would hit him that she was gone, a feeling like a sharp blow to the gut, and his stomach would seize and his eyes would burn and he'd turn away from the television set and bury his face in the cushions till the announcer's voice rose and something happened on the screen and he'd turn back to the television and the whole cycle would start over again.

Would that feeling ever go away?

Jimmy had the volume turned down low so he wouldn't disturb his mother who was sleeping upstairs. At least he hoped she was sleeping and not just staring at the ceiling like she'd been doing most of the week, like she'd lost her senses.

He was beginning to fear that his mother would never

be the same.

A light flashed behind the living room curtains and Jimmy heard his father's Buick Special pull into the driveway. He listened as the car door slammed and his father's shoe leather slapped against the concrete sidewalk.

Musial went down on strikes.

Jeez. He really was getting old.

His father stood in the foyer. "Hey buddy."

"Hey dad."

His father looked around the living room.

"Your mother in bed?"

"Uh huh."

His father set his hat atop the coat rack and took off his jacket and hung that up. He looked tired as hell.

"Who's winning?"

"Pirates. Weren't you listening to the game?"

Walt had to think about that. The game had been on the car radio, but his thoughts had been elsewhere. "How bad is it?"

"Six to two."

"Huh."

His father went down the hallway to the kitchen. Jimmy heard him in there moving things around, opening cupboards, rattling silverware. He reappeared with a can of beer and a plate of food Marie had left for him in the fridge. He sat down in the stuffed armchair and ate a piece of cold chicken leg and drank the beer. He burped from time to time, but he didn't say anything.

The Cards went down one, two, three and a cigarette commercial came on featuring Fred Flintstone and Barney Rubble.

His father finished the chicken leg and set the plate on the coffee table.

"How's school going?"

Jimmy shrugged. "Okay, I guess."

His father nodded. "I suppose it's hard...being back there."

Jimmy shrugged again. His dad drank his beer in silence. The ball game came back on. It was the top of the eighth and Briles was on the mound for St. Louis. Jimmy could feel his father's eyes on him and not on the television.

"Jim?"

"Yeah, dad?"

"Is there anything ..." His voice trailed off uncertainly.

Jimmy look at his father.

His father tried again. "Anything you can tell me about your sister. You know, that might help me understand what happened?"

Jimmy gave his dad a puzzled look. "What did happen, Dad?"

"Well, we don't know exactly. That's the thing."

"I know, but how come we don't know?"

His father made no reply. He downed the last of his beer and sat holding the empty can.

"Was your sister troubled at all?"

"By what?"

"By anything?"

Jimmy seemed to think his over. "Not that I know of."

His father stared blankly at the television. After a while he said, "You know, when I was your age..." He paused and started again. "Your grandfather always told us that family was the most important thing there is. More important than everything else. He really drilled that into us."

Jimmy nodded. He must have heard this story a dozen times. He wasn't sure if his dad forgot telling it, or if he just thought it was so important that he felt it bore repeating.

Over and over.

"I know you kids have your own lives. Lives your mother and I know nothing about. All kids do. You know what I mean, don't you, Jim?"

Jimmy squirmed. It always made him uncomfortable whenever his father talked about things other than sports. The worst was the time they started to have the sex talk and his father couldn't quite get through it. They both did a whole lot of squirming that evening. Finally, his father gave up and handed him a book and said, "Here. Read this." The book was called *The Facts of Life and Love for Teen-agers.* The print at the top of the cover said: "What Every Teen-ager Should Know," and it had a photograph of two girls and a boy sitting at a cafe counter drinking ice-cream sodas.

The book still lay in the bottom of Jimmy's sock drawer, unread.

His father continued. "When I was a teenager your grandma and grandpa, they had no idea what I was up to half the time. Or what I was going through. I'd be down at the trestle smoking cigarettes and drinking beer with my friends. They had no idea. I don't know that they much cared. They had other things to worry about. Life was a lot harder back then..."

Jimmy looked away, discomfited. It wasn't just his mother who'd been acting strange since his sister died. Jimmy wished he'd gone up to his room to do his algebra homework when he'd had the chance.

His father fell silent a moment, then he turned to Jimmy. "Did your sister have a boy she liked?"

"You mean a boyfriend?"

"Yeah. A boyfriend."

Jimmy winced. "Gee, dad. I don't know. She never talked to me about things like that."

"Well you must have heard things. Did kids ever tease

her about boys?"

Jimmy shrugged. "She liked Kenny Boyer."

"Yeah. Besides that. I mean boys. Her own age."

"Beats me, Dad."

They sat in silence a while, staring at the black and white screen. Some time passed and his father stood up and went into the kitchen and came back with another beer. Jimmy wondered where all the beer was coming from. They didn't usually keep that sort of thing in the house.

His father sat down in the armchair. "Did your sister ever talk about someone wanting to hurt her?"

"Gosh no, Dad. Not to me." Jimmy rose up on one arm. "You think somebody wanted to hurt her?"

His father shrugged. "I don't know. Probably not."

"Who'd want to hurt Em?"

"Do you know if she was mad at anyone? Or scared of anyone?"

Jimmy shook his head. "No."

"If she was going to talk to someone, tell things to, who would it have been?"

"I don't know. Mary Pat, probably."

"Mary Pat," he repeated.

"All they did was talk. All night long on the phone after you and mom went to bed."

"They did?"

"Yeah. After you went to bed Em would go downstairs and call Mary Pat and them two would be gabbing for hours. Till one o'clock, sometimes."

His father stared at him, incredulously. "I had no idea."

"Because you were asleep."

"What'd they talk about?"

Jimmy shrugged. "Girl stuff. You know. School and boys and movies."

"What boys?"

"Heck, I don't know, Dad. The boys at school, I guess."

His father stared off into space and a strange look came into his eye. "Do you think you could do me a favor?"

"Huh?"

"Could you talk to Mary Pat?"

"Me?"

"Yes. Could you do that?"

"I don't know. She don't like me. She always called me brat. She used to always tell Em 'Your brother's a real brat.'"

"That's what teenage girls do," his father said, waving his hand dismissively. "Could you talk to her for me?"

Jimmy fidgeted. "Can't *you* talk to her?"

His father seemed to think that over and shook his head. "I'd better not. But you could. You could talk to her at school, couldn't you?"

"I don't see her at school. She's a senior."

"Well you ride the bus with her, don't you?"

"Well, yeah. Sometimes. But she wouldn't talk to me on the bus. Not in front of her friends."

His father frowned at him. "Well how about after school? Or you could go over to her house?"

Jimmy couldn't even begin to imagine that. Walking over to Mary Pat Scott's house.

"I can't do that, Dad."

"Why not?"

"Because. She'd think I was crazy."

His father stared at him. Jimmy sensed he was losing his patience.

"Look, you're making this out to be a bigger deal than it is. You just walk over to her house and ask her if you can talk to her. What's she going to say? No?"

"She's going to say, what for?"

"And you say, I want to ask you about my sister."

"What about her?"

"Well, you say, Mary Pat, you were my sister's best friend. If anybody knows what happened to her it's you. You say, was there anybody who'd want to hurt her? Ask if Em ever talked about hurting herself. If she was anxious. I can write down a list of questions for you."

Jimmy sat up on the sofa. He couldn't see himself doing any of those things. The whole idea seemed crazy.

"Dad, don't make me do this," Jimmy whined. "Please."

His father fumed. "Why not?"

"Because I can't."

"Nonsense. Of course you can."

"But I don't want to."

"Oh don't be such a goddamn crybaby," his father snapped.

Jimmy turned away, stung. Then he rolled off the sofa and started toward the stairs.

"Where are you going?"

Jimmy halted at the first stair. "I got algebra homework to do," he muttered. Then he went on slowly up the stairs.

His father set down his beer can and stood up. Jimmy wondered if he was going to come after him. When he was younger his father would sometimes slip off his black leather belt and whack him smartly across and backside with it. But that hadn't happened in a good many years.

His father halted at the bottom of the staircase and called up the stairs. "For God's sakes, Jimmy, don't you want to know what happened to your sister? Don't you even care?"

Jimmy stopped at the top stair, trembling, his eyes on fire. He turned and glared angrily down at his father looming in the darkness at the bottom of the stairs.

"It won't bring her back!" Jimmy cried. He turned and

went on down the hallway. When he reached the end of the hall he stepped around Emily's cat and slammed his bedroom door and threw himself on his bed and smothered his face in his pillow.

"Nothing will," he cried.

Thirteen

Miller Drug stood on the corner of Third and Main, at the entrance to downtown, and just a brief stroll from the police station. All morning people had been phoning or stopping by the station, asking if the chief was aware that one of the front windows of the drugstore had been smashed. This annoyed Stokes. Only a blind man could have missed the broken window. Did people have such little regard for his powers of observation? He'd driven past the drugstore on his way into work and stopped to investigate, but the druggist was nowhere to be found. Stokes waited all morning for Miller to call, but hadn't heard a peep. Around noon he decided to take a walk down to the store, see what the druggist had to say.

He wouldn't have a whole lot of time. Off to the west a bank of angry, anvil-shaped clouds rose as the promised severe weather made its final approach. Above Main Street a banner snapped noisily in the wind. The banner read:

15th ANNUAL HOBO DAYS
MAY 22-24
PARADE MAY 22 7PM

As he crossed the street, Stokes found that the broken window was now covered with whitewashed plywood and the glass shards had been neatly swept away. He strode through the front doors of Miller Drug and found the druggist behind the counter of the pharmacy. Ben Miller glanced up briefly, nodded to the chief, and went back to his work. The store was empty of customers and seemed darker than usual. No doubt because of the storm rolling in. Stokes surveyed the store for other signs of mayhem and found nothing, though it was hard to see much of anything in the gloom. Miller liked to keep the lights off till late afternoon if he could get away with it. These days, with few customers, he could easily get away with it.

The druggist looked up again and said, "Chief. Something I can do for you?"

Stokes made his way across the store. He leaned an elbow on the counter and turned and nodded toward the plywood in the window.

"Looks like you had a little trouble last night."

"The window, you mean."

"Plan on filing a report?"

Ben looked up. "I don't think that will be necessary."

"No?"

"I don't think so."

"Looks to me like criminal behavior may've been involved."

"Likely an accident," said Ben flatly.

"Accident? Well sure. I suppose anything's possible. Passing truck could've kicked up a rock and tossed it through that big old plate glass window. Stranger things have happened."

Ben didn't say anything. He seemed to be waiting for Stokes to leave.

"Or maybe a deer run into the window. That happened once over in Sparta at the city bank. Big old ten-pointer. Broke his damn neck."

Stokes pulled himself off the counter and hitched up his pants. "Police report might come in handy for the insurance."

"No need to trouble yourself about that, chief."

Stokes considered the druggist a long moment.

"Uh huh," he said. "An accident then."

Ben didn't look up.

Stokes peered into the glass case beneath the counter full of antiquey brown bottles and chipped pestles and mortars. He stared at the familiar little glass bottle with the label that read "cocaine hydrochlor." The bottles and whatnot had been on display for decades. Long before Miller bought the drugstore.

However, something was missing. The green tin can of Berger's Pure Paris Green with the skeleton head and crossbones on the label. Something like that was hard to forget.

Stokes could feel the druggist's eyes studying him.

"Any who. The reason I come by is I'm doing some follow up on the death of the Ahrens girl. The one that died of arsenic poisoning about a week and a half ago."

"I'm familiar with the incident."

Across the valley thunder built up and echoed faintly off the river bluffs. Stokes glanced toward the front of the store.

"Looks like we're in for some weather."

"The farmers will be glad to hear that," Ben said vacantly. His gazed shifted back to Stokes and he waited.

"Thing is, I was wondering if you had any records of people who bought household arsenic from you in the past, oh, five or six years? That'd be right helpful."

"Household arsenic?"

"Yeah. People use the stuff to kill rats and such, don't they?"

The druggist stared at him. "We don't sell arsenic. Or anything containing arsenic."

"No?"

"Drugstores stopped carrying arsenic trioxide decades ago."

"That a fact?"

"Uh huh. Three or four decades ago, I'd say. We certainly never carried it."

Stokes jammed his hands into his back pockets. He wondered why the druggist kept saying "we" when there was only him working there. Especially since he fired the Taylor boy.

"Just out of curiosity then, where would a feller go to purchase some of that arsenic triox or whatever you called it?"

"A layman?"

"Yeah, a layman."

Ben shook his head. "I wouldn't know. I don't know why anybody would want to purchase it."

"Uh huh." It was obvious he wasn't going to get anywhere with the druggist. Stokes gazed around the store again and a flash of lightning momentarily lit up the indoors. Stokes thought about making some kind of joke about finally being able to see where he was, but he decided against it. The druggist didn't seem to be one for jokes. Instead he turned and walked over toward the soda fountain and paused beside one of the booths.

"Out of curiosity, what goes into an ice cream soda?"

"That would be ice cream and soda."

Stokes laughed. "Guess that was a silly question."

Ben made no reply.

Stokes waved his hand in the direction of the booths. "You wouldn't happen to know which one of these booths the Ahrens girl was sitting at that night?"

"Which one? I couldn't tell you. I left around eight o'clock." Ben started to come around the counter. "What is this about, chief?"

"Just curious," he said. Stokes looked down at the table and picked up the sugar container. He unscrewed the lid and shook a bit of sugar into his palm and studied it closely. He stuck out his tongue and licked a few grains.

It tasted like sugar.

Ben said, "White arsenic is tasteless, you know."

Stokes looked up. "That a fact?"

The druggist nodded.

"I guess you'd know," Stokes said. "Being a druggist and all." He turned to Ben. "You wouldn't object if I had these tested?"

"The sugar?"

"Wouldn't be too much of an imposition would it?"

Ben frowned at Stokes. "You mean with all the business we've been having?"

There he goes with the "we" again, thought Stokes. He brushed the sugar from his hands.

Ben stared at the granules on the floor. He turned and walked behind the counter and fetched a small hand broom and dustpan. He walked to where the chief had been standing and squatted down and carefully swept up the sugar.

Stokes coughed into his hand. "Sorry about that."

"The paper said those kids only had ice cream sodas that night. I can't imagine they'd put sugar in their ice cream sodas. Can you?"

Stokes shrugged. "Never know with teenagers."

A loud crack of thunder seemed to catch both men by surprise. Ben walked back behind the counter and dumped the sugar in the waste bin. "Of course I don't mind," he said. "Only, since we're going by the book I believe you'll want to secure a warrant first."

Stokes grimaced. "Come now, Mr. Miller, is that really necessary?"

"I'm a stickler for following the laws, chief. You have to be in my profession."

"Well sure." Stokes wrinkled up his face. He pulled a pack of Wrigley's chewing gum from his shirt pocket and removed a stick from the pack. He absently unwrapped the stick of gum and slid it into his mouth. "Well now. Ain't no call in bothering Judge Haynes over a little thing like this. Like you said, them kids was drinking — what was it? Ice cream sodies? Not likely they put sugar or whatnot in their sodies."

"I wouldn't think so."

Stokes nodded. "Well there you go." He looked about the darkened store and let loose a deep sigh. "Damn shame about your window. I expect those are right expensive to replace."

"Yes. I suspect so."

"Well then. Guess I'll head back for I get soaked."

"Thanks for stopping by, Chief," Ben said.

"Why sure. Give me a chance to stretch my legs."

Stokes turned and started toward the door, but halted suddenly.

"By the way. Couldn't help but notice that little can of Paris Green you kept in your display case ain't there no more."

"That's correct."

"Just wondering whatever became of it?"

"Oh. Well, it seemed...insensitive...to continue to display it. In light of recent events."

"Course," said Stokes with a nod. "Disposed of it safely, I expect?"

"The can was empty."

"Ah," said Stokes. "Well then, no worries."

"No sir."

"That's fine," said Stokes.

The police chief turned and opened the front door just as the skies opened up and a torrent of gray spring rain sheeted down on the town.

"Wouldn't you know?" Stokes said, shaking his head. He mashed his peaked cap down over his ears and pulled up his jacket collar and ducked his head and ran out into the downpour. He hadn't gone more than five steps down the flooded sidewalk, his shoes and socks soaked through, that he decided he was done investigating the Ahren's girl's death. No matter what Walt Ahrens said.

Fourteen

It was just before noon when Walt drove to the high school. He parked the Buick out front of the building and walked through the big front doors and down the corridor to the principal's office. The secretary, Mrs. Carlton, stood behind a counter talking with a small, heavy-set student. The boy, who looked fourteen or so, seemed awfully pissed off about something.

Walt waited a minute or two, then grew impatient.

"Excuse me, Sue."

"I'll be right with you, Mr. Ahrens."

"Could you just tell me which room Mary Pat Scott's in?"

Mrs. Carlton studied Walt a moment, then frowned deeply. She told the boy to sit down in one of the hard plastic chairs along the wall. The boy shuffled ill temperedly over to a chair and plopped down and crossed his arms across his chest with a loud "hmmmpf!"

"Can I help you, Mr. Ahrens?"

"Yeah. Can you tell me which room Mary Pat Scott's in?"

A flicker of confusion crossed her face. "You want to speak to Mary Pat?"

"That's right."

"May I ask why?"

Walt scowled. "Why? Because I need to talk to her."

"Is there some kind of emergency?"

"No, there's no emergency, but it's important or I wouldn't be here." Jeez, Walt thought, is this woman dense, or what?

Mrs. Carlton stared blankly at him. "Can I ask what this is about?"

"Actually, it's private."

"I see." Mrs. Carlton turned and glanced toward the principal's office. "Hold on a minute, Mr. Ahrens, I'll see if Mr. Bielawski can see you."

"Actually, Sue, I don't need to see Mr. Bielawski," Walt said, his voice growing sharp, despite himself. "I just need to know what room Mary Pat Scott is in."

Behind him the heavy-set boy began grunting and bumping his chair against the wall.

"Jeremy Helms, stop that this instant!" Mrs. Carlton cried.

The boy stilled. He harrumphed and turned his face away.

Walt glanced at the boy, thinking he could use a swift kick in his backside. He turned back to Mrs. Carlton, but she'd gone into the principal's room. "Oh for crying out loud," Walt muttered.

A moment later Mrs. Carlton returned. "Mr. Bielawski will be with you in a minute," she said and went over to her desk and sat down.

Walt cursed under his breath and shuffled over and sat beside to the Helms boy.

He looked at the kid sideways. "Bad day at Black Rock?"

The boy scowled.

"Yeah, me too," Walt said. "They got to make everything complicated. You ever notice that?"

The boy grunted, "hmmmpf!" and crossed his arms and looked away.

Presently Mr. Bielawski came out of his office. "Hello Walt," he said.

Walt turned to the boy and said, "Well, nice chatting with you." He stood up and Mr. Bielawski came around the counter to greet him.

"Hi, Jack."

They shook hands and the principal again expressed his sympathies.

"What brings you here?"

"Well, like I was telling Sue here, I just need to speak to Mary Pat Scott a minute, so if someone could just tell me where I can find her—"

"You need to speak to Mary Pat?"

"Yeah, that's what I've been saying for the past five minutes."

"Is there some kind of emergency?"

"No. I just..." Walt paused, letting his voice grow steady. "I just need to talk to her about something. It's no big deal."

"Business?"

"No. It's personal."

The principal nodded. Out in the corridor a bell rattled shrill and long. When the ring faded Bielawski said, "Can't it wait till after school?"

"Yeah, I thought about that. But you know how these kids are. All these after-school activities."

"Don't I know it," The principal said, and paused a moment. "What about calling her this evening? After she gets home?"

Walt frowned at him. "Frankly, Jack, I don't understand what the big deal is," he said testily. "I just want to talk to her for a couple of minutes."

"I understand, Walt. But we don't usually pull students out of class unless it's an emergency."

"Like I said, this will only take a few minutes."

The principal got a pained look on his face. "The other thing is we'd need a parent's permission."

"Just to talk to me?"

"Afraid so."

A flood of students swept through the hall. Walt had to raise his voice to be heard.

"What kind of nonsense is that?"

The principal lowered his voice. "Walt, some parents would get very upset if we didn't get their permission first. Not all of them, but a lot of them."

"I know the Scotts, they won't care if I talk to their daughter for a minute."

The principal shrugged. "I'd still need their permission. Rules are rules."

A small group of girls entered the principal's office and Mrs. Carlton went over to talk to them. Walt eyed them briefly. None seemed to be Mary Pat.

The principal said, "Tim's probably out on a job site, but Gale might be home. I could try to call her, I guess."

"Fine," Walt said through clinched teeth.

"Okay." The principal turned back toward his office and abruptly halted. "If she asks what you want to talk to Mary Pat about?"

"Just say I want to ask her about my daughter."

"Anything in particular?"

"No," Walt said, his voice tight.

The principal nodded and stepped into his office. Walt turned and sat down again beside the Helms kid.

The boy immediately let out a loud, rotten fart. The girls turned around and giggled. One said, "Ewww, gross!"

Walt rolled his eyes and stood up. He walked over to a large window that looked out on the corridor and sighed and began to study a sports calendar taped to the glass. The high school varsity boys' baseball schedule. Then his eyes fell on a photo on the trophy case across from the principal's office. It was Emily's yearbook photo from last year. Above the picture, in red Magic Marker, were the words, "We miss you, Emily!"

"Sorry, Walt. Mrs. Scott said no."

Walt turned. "Oh for the love of Pete!"

The principal looked past Walt to the Helms boy

thrashing about on one of the chairs.

"What are you doing here, Jeremy?" he said.

"Mrs. Hill sent me here."

Walt cut off the principal. "What'd she say?"

"She said she did not want you talking to Mary Pat."

"That's it?"

"Yes."

"Did you tell her why I wanted to talk to her?"

"I said you wanted to ask her something about..." He glanced toward the girls at the counter, and said, "Your daughter."

Walt stared hard at the principal.

"Excuse me!" said a female student. Walt stepped aside as the group of girls exited the office.

"Why don't you call over there this evening?" the principal said. "Maybe they'll change their mind if you talk to them."

Christ almighty. It was such a simple request.

"Thanks for the advice," Walt growled and turned and stormed out the door.

He walked into the corridor, over to the trophy case. As he drew closer he found that some little piece of shit had drawn a thin curly mustache on his daughter's upper lip. He tore the photograph off the case and ripped it to shreds. Then he dropped the pieces on the floor and turned and found Jack Bielawski and Mrs. Carlton staring at him from the principal's office, both wearing a look of confusion mixed with pity. Walt colored, then he stooped, picked up the scraps of paper, and carried them with him out the front doors.

Fifteen

Normally Rachel Miller would have stopped by the Gideon A&P for her weekly supply of wine and spirits — it would've been a lot closer to home, not to say cheaper — but she'd grown tired of the checkout lady's judgmental looks, even when Rachel loaded the cart with extra groceries she didn't need. "Having a diner party?" the checkout woman would say with a bogus grin. "No," Rachel would respond, returning the fake smile.

Screw that. She'd go to the liquor store outside of town where the old man who owned the store was always happy to see an attractive young woman and didn't judge.

Rachel had just pulled into the lot of Newsome's West End Liquor Store when the thunderstorm hit. She sat behind the wheel finishing her cigarette, the window cracked a half-inch and a fine mist of spray finding its way inside to settle on her face and hands. The radio played the top of the hour news, a story about the foreign ministers of Britain, France, the Soviet Union and the United States meeting in Geneva for some conference on the reunification of Germany, then something about Elizabeth Taylor marrying Eddie Fischer. Another scandal and another Jewish husband. Rachel wondered how many goys knew that Liz had converted to Judaism. She turned off the radio and stabbed out the cigarette in the ashtray and blew smoke toward the opening in the window. She hadn't thought to bring her umbrella, so she removed a polka dotted scarf from her purse and wrapped the scarf around her head and opened the door and made a run for the front door.

The doorbells clanged as she entered and Al Newsome glanced up from his stool behind the counter and his mouth widened in a closed-mouth grin. He wore thick heavy rimmed glasses and a white short-sleeved shirt and gray slacks, the same uniform he wore pretty much every day. A staticky ball game played on a portable radio on a shelf behind him.

"Hullo Misses Miller," he said. "Quite the storm we are having."

Rachel glanced around the store. The shop was tiny but well stocked for a small town liquor store. Rachel was pleased to find she was the only customer.

"No umbrella, huh?"

"I forgot, silly me," she said.

"I'd offer you mine but I seem to have misplaced it."

"That's sweet," she said.

He slid off the stool and looked at her with rheumy eyes. "Three bottles of cabernet?"

"And a fifth of Beefeater, please."

"Coming right up."

As Newsome shuffled down the counter toward the hard liquor, a blast of wind slammed a sheet of heavy rain against the store windows and the radio crackled and faded in and out.

Rachel lifted herself up on her toes and hummed anxiously, a Miles Davis tune.

"Feller came in this morning and mentioned there was a window out at the drugstore," Newsome said.

"Excuse me?"

Newsome took down a bottle of Beefeater and turned to Rachel. "You ain't heard?"

Rachel stiffened. "No."

"Oh," said Newsome. He set the gin on the counter and went to fetch the wine.

"This feller said one of the big plate glass windows was busted out. I'm surprised you ain't heard."

Rachel took a deep breath and pressed her lips

together.

Newsome pulled four brown paper bags from under the counter and bagged the bottles and slipped them into a larger brown bag. "Comes to a sawbuck even," he said.

Rachel opened her purse and found a ten in her billfold and handed it to Newsome. She hefted the bag.

"Sorry to be the bearer of bad news," he said, placing the bill in the register.

"That's all right, Mr. Newsome," she said. "You have a good day."

"You too. Don't get too wet," he said, settling back on his stool.

Rachel hurried out to the Fairlane. She eased behind the wheel and tossed the scarf onto the passenger side seat. She sat fuming and watching as the rain turned suddenly to hail. Small pea-sized balls of ice hammered and popped on the roof and the hood of the Ford making little dents in the steel.

Was he going to tell her about the vandalism or did he think she was so cut off from the outside world that she wouldn't find out?

Rachel reached into the bag and brought out the bottle of Beefeater. She cracked the seal and took a long swig. Not very ladylike, but fuck it. She returned the bottle to the bag and started the Ford and pulled out onto the highway. She headed west toward downtown.

The wipers slapped noisily as the Fairlane motored blindly through the storm. She drove right through an intersection near the grade school, completely failing to see the stop sign. To her left, someone blasted a horn. Rachel swallowed hard and white knuckled the steering wheel and drove on.

As she approached Third Street the drugstore came into view. The store looked dark inside. Like it was closed. No cars out front either. A sheet of white plywood covered one of the front plate glass windows. Rachel hit the brakes and pulled in front of the store, parking before the broken window.

The hail had stopped, but the rain fell steadily. Rachel wrapped the scarf about her head again and eased out of the car and walked briskly to the door. The overhead bell tinkled as she entered.

She shook the rain from her scarf.

The store was empty save her husband who sat hunched at the counter, his back to her. His lab coat lay on the stool beside him. He slowly dragged a spoon around in a mug of coffee.

Ben cocked his head as his wife entered. He folded up a piece of paper and slipped it into his shirt pocket. He turned back to his coffee.

"Ben, what happened?"

Ben held silent.

"Ben?"

"Yeah?"

"What happened?"

Ben set down the spoon with a soft clink.

"Ben, I'm talking to you. What happened to our window?"

"It broke."

"It broke?" Rachel walked over and sat down on the stool beside him. He kept his eyes focused somewhere back of the counter. "Windows do not just break. Windows are broken. By people. Often by anti-Semites."

"Don't start," he said wearily.

"Don't start? Ben, people are breaking our windows and you tell me not to start? When do I start? When they come to lynch us? Then I start?"

"Nobody's going to lynch anybody," Ben said. Then, almost inaudibly, he said, "They're just scared."

"They're scared? It's goddamn Kristallnacht in here

and you say they're scared?"

Ben studied his wife. He couldn't tell if she'd been drinking — she could hide it well — but he assumed she had.

"Quit exaggerating."

"Ben, when were you going to tell me about this?"

He braced himself for the usual "why oh why had he dragged her to this godforsaken cultural swamp," followed by his same old response. She'd agreed to it. She'd wanted her husband to own his own drugstore, not have to work for his Uncle Jake all his life, and this store in this town was all they could afford.

Was it his fault he liked Gideon? That he enjoyed living in a small Midwestern town with normal, average people, picnics and parades and front porch swings? Besides Rachel exaggerated Gideon's backwardness. Sure it was southern Illinois. Sure it was a rural county, but it wasn't the Jim Crow South. They didn't lynch Negroes here. Or Jews for that matter. They never had, as far as he could tell. And weren't they only ninety minutes from the city? Didn't they go back every Saturday for temple?

So he felt a little guilty, but wasn't Rachel's problem that she was too wrapped up in herself? What she needed was to try thinking about others, the less fortunate. How many times had he suggested she join some civic group that helped the poor? He himself had joined the Chamber of Commerce, the Rotary Club, the Kiwanis. (He tried to join the Elks, but was discretely told that they didn't allow Jews.) Not Rachel. According to her the women's charities were all run by crazy fundamentalist Protestant women's groups and she wouldn't be welcomed. So why bother?

"I'm not going to give them the satisfaction of turning me down because of my religion. Or my race. Or whatever the hell it is they hate about us," she'd told Ben.

Now Rachel glanced at him with gin-inflamed eyes

that melted his spine.

"I'm asking you, Ben, when were you going to tell me?"

The truth was he was never going to tell her. Not if he could get away with it. He didn't think this had anything to do with anti-Semitism. How would that even be possible? People in Gideon had no experience with Jews, good or bad. Just with him and is wife, and his wife not so much. Besides the people seemed to like him. His drugstore was a popular nightspot.

Had been, anyway.

How then did you explain the loss of business? The brick through the window. Yes, it had been a brick and not some accidental stone kicked up by a car tire. A paver with a note tied with a piece of twine.

It made no sense. Sure people were scared. The girl had been at the soda fountain three hours before she died.

Ben wasn't naïve. He'd experienced anti-Semitism his whole life growing up in St. Louis. Hell, when he was twelve, one of the "unofficial" events during middle school spirit week had been "Hit a Jew Day." There were only a handful of Jews in the school then, most of them girls, so Ben would get quite the pummeling. The school administrators were told about it, but they naturally turned a blind eye.

Ben started to say, "What do you want me to do?" but he knew what she wanted him to do. Sell out and move back to St. Louis. Back to the little Jewish settlement that was University City. Back to Gaslight Square and Powell Symphony Hall and the Fox Theater and the Two Cents Plain kosher deli and their family and friends.

"This is just the beginning, you know," Rachel said. "You think they'll stop with breaking windows? Did the Germans stop with breaking windows? They did not stop, Ben. And these people, all of them, they're Germans."

"They're not Germans."

"No? Eggemeyer? Schulz? Esterhage? Mueller? Ahrens?"

Ben turned away. He was surprised she knew so many of the local names, considering she hardly ever left the house. "What do you want me to do? Sell out? Go home with my tail between my legs? Beg Uncle Jacob for my old job back?"

"It wouldn't be like that, Ben. It isn't like we failed. We just missed our families. Missed the city. Our own kind. We weren't cut out for the boondocks."

Ben understood. She wasn't afraid of rednecks. She just wanted to move back to St. Louis. It wouldn't have surprised him if Rachel herself hadn't lobbed that brick through the window.

Ben steeled himself. "This is our home, Rachel. No one's driving us away."

Rachel glowered at him. Suddenly she reached out and snatched the piece of paper from Ben's shirt pocket. She turned away on the stool and opened it.

"Get out Jew!"

She stood up slowly, her face an ashen gray. She held the open paper up in front of him. "What else are you keeping from me?"

Ben looked down. "Nothing."

Rachel shook her head slowly. She wadded up the piece of paper and threw it at Ben. It bounced off his chest and fell to the floor. Then she turned and ran across the store, out through the front door and into the pouring rain.

Sixteen

The main story in the *Herald-Tribune* that week concerned the upcoming Hobo Days Picnic and Parade. According to the paper, five hundred people were expected in town for the three-day event:

> Fans of the comic hero Boxcar Frank, king of the hobos, will celebrate his 47th birthday with a hobo-themed picnic and parade this weekend in the hometown of his creator. It's the 15th year of Hobo Days. As many as 1,000 people once attended the event in creator Hal Keen's hometown of Gideon, many donning the raiment of hobo royalty, but those numbers have dwindled to just a few hundred in recent years.
>
> But picnic organizers say they hope those numbers will rebound this year.
>
> "If anybody's come before, they need to come back because it's really going to be great," picnic chairman Harvey Gilster said. "It's a big family picnic this year. We have so much going on."

Readers hoping for a follow-up to the Ahrens girl's death were disappointed. The editor had made the rounds, talked with the sheriff, the police chief, the coroner, but there was simply nothing new to add.

Nor was there anything in the paper about the drugstore's broken window. When Norris asked the chief about that, Stokes simply shrugged and said the druggist told him it must've been a stray rock kicked up by a tire.

"So, no police report then?"

"Nope."

"What do *you* think happened?"

"No comment."

Norris frowned at the chief. "I'm going to start calling you Chief 'No Comment' Stokes."

"I don't know, I kind of like the sound of that," Stokes said.

~ ~ ~

That evening Walt found Marie sitting alone, shivering on the back porch, a tear-stained letter balled up in her hand. Walt pulled up a lawn chair and sat down beside her. Above the neighboring rooftops the clear sky darkened to slate and shadows stretched along the yard. The still air hummed with gnats and mosquitoes. Fireflies blinked over the backyards.

He watched her a while and sighed with sorrow for her and said, "Kind of cold out here to be without a jacket, ain't it hon?"

Marie dried her eyes with her apron and looked at her husband.

"I was about to go in. Get your dinner heated up."

Somewhere a dog began barking.

"What you got there?" he said, indicating the letter.

"This came in the mail today."

"What is it?"

"A letter for Em."

Walt held silent a moment.

"Who's it from?"

"The university."

"Oh."

Marie lowered her gaze. "She was accepted into the teacher's program."

Walt hunched forward and brushed away a mosquito buzzing around his eyes.

Marie said, "She could've started college in the fall."

Walt pressed his lips together and he gently took his

wife's hand. He looked away, a catch in his throat, but his eyes remained dry and hard. He felt wooden inside like one of those cigar store Indians.

Walt gazed at the letter, wet and crumpled in his wife's hand. Emily would've been the first person in his family — or Marie's family for that matter — to attend college. He hadn't thought it possible. She seemed so young and immature for her age. She'd been an average student at best, far as he could tell. Not that he'd paid much attention to her grades. That was Marie's job. She signed the report cards, attended the parent-teacher conferences. If pressed, he would've guessed she was a B student. B minus. Anything worse and he would've heard about it, like when Jimmy got that D in algebra last fall.

"She loved kids. She would've been a wonderful teacher," Marie said, choking back tears.

Walt nodded. It came back to him now, why Emily had wanted to go into teaching. When Marie was fourteen she'd gotten a scholarship to attend the Normal School. Back then, that was a big deal. The parish priest had even come over to the house one snowy February evening to deliver the good news. Marie's father thanked the priest, but he refused to allow Marie to accept the scholarship. Young girls of fourteen didn't just tramp off to school in some far corner of the state. It was unseemly. Besides, she was needed on the farm. The priest was disappointed, but said he understood. Anne tried to talk to her husband, a typical hardheaded German, tried to get him to change his mind. But he wouldn't discuss it.

Marie remained on the farm, and four years later she married one of the Ahrens boys from town she'd known from grade school. In the end, her father got four more years of free labor out of her.

Walt carefully removed the letter from Marie's grasp before it was completely ruined. She might want to put the letter in a scrapbook someday. He smoothed the letter and laid it on a small patio table.

There was something Walt had been wanting to ask Marie for days, but she'd always seemed too fragile to broach it. She was still frail, but he felt like he couldn't leave off any longer.

"Hon, I've got to ask you something."

She studied him, her eyes questioning.

"Do you think there's any chance that Em ..."

His resolve weakened and his voice trailed off.

"That she what?"

Walt swallowed hard. Out with it, he thought.

"Well...that she'd take her own life?"

He waited, prepared for any kind of horrible outburst. Marie slowly turned away and stared into the distance.

She hadn't gone to pieces. That was good.

"No," she said, her lips pressed firmly together. "She would never...not my little girl." Then she looked at Walt and her eyes seemed to waver. Her head fell against his chest. Walt could feel hot tears soaking through his shirt. "Oh, Walt, I don't know," she wailed.

Walt nodded and stroked his wife's hair. He looked off over the backyard.

"It's okay."

He held her for a long time. The shadows were complete now and the hum of cicadas echoed from branches and rose to a high fevered pitch and then faded.

Walt said, "I've been thinking it over. I want to hire an investigator."

Marie stiffened. "You what?"

"An investigator. Someone to look into all this."

Marie's hands flew up to her throat like scared birds. "Oh Walt, no ..."

That was pretty much the reaction he'd expected.

Walt held firm. "Now Marie, I've made up my mind."

She turned away.

"You've heard what the police said. They're not going to do a goddamn thing."

She became silent and could hear the cry of crickets and caws of crows from blackened trees.

"If we don't do something, nobody will."

"Please Walt."

Walt glared impatiently at his wife. "What's the matter with you? Don't you want to know what happened to our little girl?"

"No, I—"

"No?"

"I mean, I did, but I don't any more. Please Walt, let it go. Can't you see that I've let it go?"

"Actually, no, I can't."

"Well I have. It took me a while, but I did. I let *her* go. I let going of not knowing. Walt, honey, I've prayed and prayed on this and the Lord spoke to me. He told me I didn't have to know."

"The Lord told you that?"

"Yes. He told me Em's all right. She's with Him. She's found peace. And now I've found peace." Her voice cracked with emotion. "All this will do is bring it all back. The pain and sadness. Please, Walt."

"You don't act like you've found peace."

"I know, but I have."

Walt stood up and glared down at her. "Well I'm glad you found peace, Marie, but I haven't. I've got to know. I tried doing this myself, but I can't. I don't know how. People won't talk to me."

Marie looked down at the porch floor. Walt could see she was shutting down, that he was losing her.

"You don't have to have anything to do with this, Marie. In fact, I'm sorry I told you. I'm sorry I upset you, but it doesn't change a thing. I'm going to see a man in

East St. Louis tomorrow."

He felt they were coming apart. That's what tragedy did to families. It weakened them till they lacked the strength to remain whole. A family was like a chain and Emily was the missing link. And once that link was gone you could never replace it.

Seventeen

Walt was up early Friday morning and slipped out of the house without saying a word to Marie. On the way out of town he stopped by the dealership and left a note for Harvey saying he'd be in around noon.

He had found Martin Duggan in the East St. Louis phone book under A-1 Investigations, the first listing under private investigators.

If he's smart enough to be first in the phone book he's probably smart enough to hire. That's what Walt figured anyway.

He rolled into East St. Louis around nine-thirty and drove around another twenty minutes till he located the office. He must have driven by the place four or five times before he found it, a nondescript office wedged into a row of somewhat seedy storefronts two blocks from downtown, next to the Oddfellow's Hall and across the street from a fire station. Walt parallel parked the Buick a block away and slipped an accordion folder under his arm and hurried toward the office. He was twenty minutes late.

The sign on the glass door read A-1 Investigations and Bail Bonds. He stepped inside and quickly closed the door. The office could have doubled as a walk-in closet, barely enough room for two desks and some dented file cabinets. No windows either. A single florescent bulb buzzed and flickered on the ceiling. The flooring consisted of dirty cracked tiles.

"Hello?" Walt said.

A toilet flushed in the rear of the office and a back door opened and a guy with the build of a failed boxer and the face of a man who'd seen things came out adjusting his pants.

"Ahrens?" the man said, looking him over.

"Yes."

The man extended his hand, which Walt took reluctantly. "Martin Duggan. Call me Marty. See you found the place."

"Yeah. Took a bit of detective work." Walt laughed faintly.

Duggan gave him a blank look. "Please, sit," he said, indicating one of the three yellow vinyl chairs. Walt chose the least dirty chair, while Duggan took a seat behind one of the desks. He slipped a handkerchief from his coat pocket and loudly blew his nose. "So, you were saying on the phone that your daughter passed away recently."

"Two weeks ago."

"My sympathies."

Walt nodded. The roar of a filling toilet tank drifted into the little room. From the sound of it something must have gotten stuck.

"Arsenic, wasn't it?"

"Correct."

"And there was a coroner's jury?"

"Yeah," Walt said irritably. "Completely worthless. They said the manner of death was undetermined."

"Undetermined?"

He nodded.

"And you think what? She was a victim of a homicide? Foul play?"

"I don't know."

He looked like a garbage man, Walt thought. Or maybe the guy who owns a garbage dump. Duggan's hair was black and uncombed. He had a small mouth with thin lips and a button chin and he wore a white pin-stripped shirt with visible sweat stains under the armpits.

I'm not hiring him for his looks, Walt reminded himself.

"You don't know?" said Duggan.

"All I know is nothing makes any sense."

Duggan looked confused, so Walt tried again. "I just want to understand what happened to my daughter, that's all. I just want the truth. I mean, we know what she died of, but we don't know why. I want to know why. You know what I mean?"

"What do the police say? What do they think happened?"

"Stokes? He doesn't know his ass from his elbow."

"He didn't investigate?"

"He says there's no evidence a crime's been committed, so he can't do a goddamn thing. Did you ever hear such bullshit?"

"So the cops are telling you to drop it?"

"Pretty much."

Duggan stood up and walked back to the toilet. Walt could hear him jiggling the handle, to no avail. He slammed the bathroom door and walked back to his desk. "And you say your daughter wasn't having the blues or nothing like that?"

Walt shook his head.

"And there wasn't no one wanting to hurt her or hurt any one in the family?"

"No, no. Not that I'm aware of."

"But you're not positive?"

"I mean, I don't have anybody pissed off at me and I sure can't imagine Emily did."

"You said you own a car dealership."

"I have a business partner, but yes. Why?"

"You repossess cars?"

"Sure. Every once in a while."

"So how do you know—?"

Walt leaned forward and cut him off. "Look. You repossess a vehicle, somebody calls and cusses you out.

Once a guy fired a shotgun into the air, but that was the worst that happened. They sure as hell don't poison your daughter."

Duggan nodded. "And there's no way she could've taken it accidentally? No arsenic around the house?"

"Of course not."

"You checked?"

"Yes, I checked."

Duggan removed a toothpick from his shirt pocket and slipped it into his mouth, rolling it from one side to the other. "What you got there?" he said, indicating the accordion folder.

Walt drummed his fingers against the folder. "Newspaper clips. Coroner's report. Transcripts from the coroner's jury. Some notes I made after talking to people. And my daughter's diary and some of her letters. I was thinking a set of fresh eyes might see something I missed."

"Could be," Duggan said. He took the folder from Walt and peered inside at the contents. He removed Emily's diary and studied the broken lock.

"I did that," Walt said.

Duggan gave him a look.

"After...she passed away."

Duggan nodded and flipped open the diary to a random page.

Walt leaned forward, his hands folded under his chin, and waited. A siren started up just outside. Walt turned and looked across the street as a fire engine pulled out of the station. Duggan didn't seem to notice.

At length Duggan closed the book and looked at Walt and raised his voice over the siren. "So you read this?"

"Some of it."

"But not all of it?"

"As much as I could stand."

"And?"

Walt shrugged. "Pretty normal stuff, I guess. For a teenage girl. I mean as far as I can tell."

Duggan nodded and laid the diary on his desk next to a stack of other papers. He leaned back in his chair and folded his hands across his stomach and looked at Walt.

"So here's what I can tell you, Mr. Ahrens. It ain't unusual for women — teenage girls I mean — to take poison. If a dame — a girl — wants to kill herself, it's usually an overdose of pills or poison."

Walt stared silently.

"On the other hand, poison is a real easy way to murder someone. Easy to slip into someone's soup or drink. And arsenic, it looks just like sugar and don't taste like nothing. Or maybe that's strychnine? I get the two confused. Anyway, it's hard to diagnose. You get some country sawbones, he's going to think it's a stomach bug."

Duggan saw Walt flinch.

"Is that what happened?"

Walt shifted in his seat. "Look, Mr. Duggan—"

"Call me Marty."

"Marty. I understand all that. All these theories. Conjecture. I've heard it all. I don't need more conjecture. I just need to know how this happened. Everyone keeps telling me to let it go, that we'll never know what happened. But I can't believe that. Goddamn it, somebody knows what happened."

Duggan scratched at an armpit. "Sure, Mr. Ahrens. I get it." Duggan thought for a moment. "Let me ask you something. The car dealership. Is business good? Run into any financial troubles recently?"

"Yes, business is good. Why do you ask?"

"Any debt?"

"No. Just the mortgage on our house."

"What about insurance? Have you taken out any policies on your children?"

Walt scowled. "Of course not."

"Can you verify that?"

Walt started to his feet. "What the hell is this?"

"Sit down, Mr. Ahrens. You want me to investigate this or not?"

"You're working for me, not investigating me!"

"I ain't working for you yet. And I won't be if you ain't going to cooperate."

Walt sat down, seething.

Duggan opened a desk drawer and pulled out a notepad and pen and tossed them onto the desk. He flipped through the pad till he found an empty page. "So Wallace. Do I call you Wallace? Wally?"

Walt frowned at him. "Walter. My name's Walter. You can call me Walt."

"Sorry. Walt. So Walt, tell me this. Who do you suspect?"

"Who do I suspect?"

"Yeah. You must suspect someone?"

"I...I don't know."

Duggan nodded. "You don't know?"

Walt shook his head. "I—"

"Okay. The first thing we do is we draw up a list of suspects. Let's start at the beginning. Who was the last person to see your daughter...Emily, right? Who was the last person to see Emily alive?"

"Well, there were a lot of us. Me ... my wife ... the doctors. Our son."

Duggan waved this off. "Okay Walt. Here's what I need you to do. I need you to draw me up a list of suspects. And a list of people I need to talk to. Police chief, coroner. I'll definitely need to talk to your business partner."

"Why?"

"Walt, you want me to investigate this fully or you want me to half-ass it?"

"Well, obviously—"

"Can you get me that list?"

"Yeah. Sure."

"Fine then. I charge twenty-five bucks a day, plus expenses, that includes motel if I need to stay down there. And I'll definitely need to stay down there. And I'll need a fifty-dollar retainer."

Walt swallowed hard and nodded. "Okay." He took out his checkbook and set it on his thigh and wrote out a check. He handed the check to Duggan.

Duggan shoved the piece of paper into his shirt pocket and stood up and extended his hand. "Good. I enjoy a challenge."

Walt got up and took Duggan's hand. He wasn't exactly sure what Duggan meant by enjoying a challenge.

Walt paused. "So, now what?"

Duggan stepped around his desk and rested his hand on Walt's shoulder and escorted him toward the door. "Don't worry about a thing, Wally. I'm on the case. You'll be hearing from me soon."

The door rattled shut behind him.

Outside the street was busy with shoppers, high-heeled women going into the bank, the beauty shop, the five and dime store. A bus rolled by, spewing thick clouds of exhaust. There were more Negroes than the last time Walt was in town, or so it seemed. He looked up and down the street trying to remember where he parked the Buick. He had no idea, so started walking south.

He walked past the car twice before he remembered what he was even looking for.

Eighteen

Behind his desk Stokes had removed his socks and was working on his toenails with a large pair of office scissors. The nails were thick and horny looking. Even he disliked looking at them.

Mrs. Campbell poked her head inside the door and gave the chief a start.

"A Mr. Duggan would like a word with you," she said. Then louder, "He doesn't have an appointment."

Stokes was relieved she couldn't see behind the desk.

Mrs. Campbell looked at Stokes and knitted her brow in consternation. "Are you cutting them horny old toenails again?"

"You don't need to know everything I—"

"Disgusting!"

Stokes sighed and dropped the scissors and his sock into a bottom drawer and slammed the drawer. He slipped his naked foot into his shoe.

"What'd you say his name was?" he shouted.

"Duggan."

Stokes shook his head and muttered, "I don't know any Duggans."

"That's because he isn't from around here."

Stokes opened the drawer and took out his sock and tried to slip it on quickly without Mrs. Campbell noticing. "What's he selling?"

Mrs. Campbell stepped inside the office and lowered her voice. "It's about the Ahrens girl."

"Oh, for the love of Pete."

"He's a private investigator. I could say you're busy pruning your feet."

"Funny." Stokes slid the sock over his foot and slipped

his foot back into his shoe. Then he bent over and tied the lace. "No," he grunted. "Send him in. We'll give him ten minutes, then interrupt us. You know the drill."

Mrs. Campbell nodded and walked back to the outer office.

Stokes lifted his eyes. A dark, greasy looking man stood before him, his meaty hand outstretched. Stokes noticed the dark red stain on his striped tie.

"Chief Stokes? I'm Martin Duggan, A-1 Investigations." They shook hands and Duggan handed the chief a dog-eared business card.

"How do you do?" Stokes said. Stokes glanced briefly at the card and started to slip it into his shirt pocket. "Checking in, huh?"

"That's right. You mind if I have that back?"

"Hmm? Oh, sure." Stokes returned the card. "Understand you're here about the Ahrens girl?"

"That's right."

"Walt Ahrens hire you?"

"Well, that's confidential, chief. You understand. But yeah."

"Well, take a load off." Stokes sat down and studied the private eye. He didn't much care for his looks. He looked like a garbage man in a thrift store suit. He could smell his sweaty armpits from across the desk.

"Walt's a good friend," Stokes said. "We go back a long ways. Course I was a few years ahead of him in school."

Duggan stared silently at the chief. He withdrew a pen and notepad from his coat pocket and clicked the pen.

Stokes continued, "Thing is, Walt's taken this real hard, losing his daughter. Both him and Marie. Frankly I'm worried about them. The whole town is. You ask me, what that family needs is spiritual counseling, not a private dick. No offense."

Duggan didn't say anything.

Stokes picked up a pencil and tapped it on his desk a few times. He looked at Duggan who seemed to be waiting for the chief to finish whatever it was he was trying to say.

"Okay Mr. Duggan. I don't have a whole lot of time. How can I be of assistance?"

"I understand there's no ongoing investigation?"

"Well now, I don't know what your experience with law enforcement is, but rest assured if we come across any evidence of wrongdoing we'll investigate."

"The girl was poisoned."

"She did ingest poison, yes."

"You think it was an accident?"

Stokes cracked his knuckles one at a time. "We had us a coroner's inquest a few days ago. Too bad you missed it."

"I got the transcripts."

"Uh huh. Then you know the jury come back with a finding of undetermined. I don't see no reason to question their decision."

"Or lack of a decision."

"Same thing."

Duggan rubbed his chin stubble. "Off the record, then."

"Off the record?"

"No hunches?"

"I keep my hunches to myself."

Duggan took this in, his head slightly bowed, his shoulders slumped. "Okay, chief. What can you tell me about Walt Ahrens?"

Stokes made a point of looking at his watch. "Other than what I already told you, not much. Walt grew up here. He's a World War II vet. Runs a successful car dealership with Harv Gilster, who I believe is his second cousin. Hell, Walt might be my second cousin, for that matter. Maybe third. Anyway, he married a nice local girl. Two kids. Course one now. Involved in the community.

Member of the school board. Or maybe he isn't any more. Chamber. Lions Club. All that. Well respected. Like I said, he's taken this hard. You ask me, what he needs most of all is to move on with his life. Put this behind him."

"You wouldn't happen to know if Mr. Ahrens took out a life insurance policy on his daughter?"

Stokes' voice hardened. "You're talking about Walt Ahrens."

"It's a standard question in a poisoning case. You must've looked into it."

"Where'd you say you were from again?"

"A-1 Investigations."

"No. The town?"

"East St. Louis."

Stokes shifted his weight in the chair. "To answer your question, I don't know."

Duggan made a couple of lines in a notepad. Stokes wondered what the hell was keeping Mrs. Campbell.

"If you ask me you're wasting your time here. If Walt hired you I suspect it's because people are tired of answering his questions. But people around here don't really take to strangers. You ain't likely to get any more information than Walt did."

"I thought I'd go over and talk to the druggist."

"Waste of time," said Stokes. "I already talked to him. Complete waste of time."

"Looks like something happened to his window. That new?"

"Could've been a truck kicked up a rock. Maybe a deer run into it."

"A deer, huh?"

Stokes shrugged. "Happened over in Sparta not too long ago."

Duggan looked down at his notepad. "One last thing, chief, if you don't mind."

142

Stokes shrugged.

"Anything like this ever happened before? Here, I mean. A poison case? A young girl turning up dead out of the blue?"

Stokes pretended to think this over. "Nope. Can't say as I recall any such thing."

"Uh huh." Duggan stood up. "Well, I thank you for your time."

"Sure. Next time you might call ahead. Make an appointment."

"I'll do that." Duggan turned toward the door, but hesitated. "Oh, say chief, is there a decent hotel in town?"

"Staying on then, eh? Well, there's a motel that ain't too bad. The Riverside over on Route 3. You passed it on the way in."

Duggan nodded.

"Nice cafe next door though. The Family Diner. Samantha makes a fine pot roast. Highly recommended."

Duggan turned toward the door. "Thanks, chief. It's been very enlightening."

"Why sure," said Stokes. "If you're looking for something to do while you're in town, Hobo Days kicks off tonight. Be folks from all over come in for that. Far away as St. Louis. Parade starts at seven o'clock."

"Yeah. Well thanks for the tip."

"Don't mention it."

Stokes heard Duggan say goodbye to Mrs. Campbell and the front door close behind him. He peered out the door and saw Mrs. Campbell sitting at her desk. Then he opened his desk drawer and took out the pair of scissors and kicked off his left shoe. He had just removed his black sock with the large hole in the heel when he heard Mrs. Campbell say, "Are you cutting your toenails again?"

He looked up and found her standing in his doorway. "You need something?" he said.

Mrs. Campbell shook her head and turned away. "Disgusting."

"You sound like a broken record," Stokes said, kicking off his other shoe.

Nineteen

Duggan stood in the showroom of Ahrens and Gilster Auto Sales gazing at a bright yellow Volkswagen Beetle, trying to understand what kind of person would buy such a monstrosity. A man in a checked sport coat and a thin black tie peered at him from his office doorway and stepped outside to greet him.

"Fine little import," the man said.

"Uh huh," Duggan said. "You wouldn't happen to be Harvey Gilster?"

"I sure am. And you are?"

"Marty Duggan, private investigator. I called earlier." Duggan took a business card from his wallet and offered it to Harvey.

The card was dog-eared and had a dark smudge mark on it. Harvey studied the card briefly and started to slip it into his jacket pocket.

"Mind if I have that back?"

"Hmm? Oh sure," Harvey said returning the card. "This isn't going to take long is it?"

"Shouldn't. Is there some place we can talk?"

"My office."

Duggan followed Harvey across the small showroom. He was impressed that they sold real automobiles, coupes and sedans, and not just pick'em up trucks.

"Is Ahrens around?" Duggan said.

"I believe he's on the phone. You need to talk to him?"

"No. Just wondering."

They stepped into the office and Harvey closed the door. "Have a seat."

Duggan pulled up a chair and plopped down on the vinyl seat cushion, which made a distinct fart-like sound as it expelled air. Both men ignored this.

"So I spoke to Walt," Harvey said. "He says you're investigating his daughter's death and you had some questions."

"That's right."

"Well, if it's okay with Walt, I guess it's okay."

Duggan brought his fist to his mouth and fought a belch.

"But I'll tell you up front, I don't like it," Harvey continued. "I think what Walt needs is to get on with his life and stop...you know, dwelling on what happened. It isn't healthy, if you ask me."

Duggan shrugged. "Mr. Gilster, I know you're busy, so what say we get down to brass tacks?"

Harvey folded his hands. "Suits me."

"Fine. I need to know if Mr. Ahrens has been having any financial problems."

"You worried his checks won't clear?"

Duggan grinned like it hurt. "Seriously. Is Ahrens a gambling man or anything like that? He got any major debts I should know about?"

Harvey shook his head. "He might play a little five-card stud with the boys on poker night, but that's as far as that goes."

"So he never mentioned anything about money troubles?"

"Not Walt. Wouldn't even if he had them."

Duggan nodded. "And the dealership is in good shape financially?"

Harvey squirmed a little in his seat. "We're doing all right. This is kind of a boom time for automobile purchases."

"No large sums of money unaccounted for?"

"No sir. We run a pretty tight ship."

"You're sure?"

Harvey scowled. "Sure I'm sure." He studied Duggan. Not even two minutes and the guy had already gotten on his nerves. "If you don't mind me saying, mister, it sounds like you're investigating Walt."

Duggan smiled at that. "A good PI always starts by ruling out the person who hires him. That's the way these things work."

"That doesn't make a whole lot of sense to me. Why would someone with something to hide hire an investigator?"

"Prove they got nothing to hide."

"So I guess you wouldn't hire a *good* investigator."

Duggan made a wry grimace and ignored the slight. "Ahrens ever had any trouble with the law?"

"Not that I ever heard. And trust me, I would've heard."

"How about his family? Any troubles there that you know of? Other than the daughter's death, I mean?"

Harvey shook his head. "No more than any other family. Less than most. They're good people, the Ahrenses. Marie is a lovely woman and Jimmy's a fine boy."

"Uh huh. And the daughter?"

"She was a beautiful person. Caring, smart, loved baseball. Her father's pride and joy."

"The Norman Rockwells, huh?"

"What?"

"All American family."

"Pretty much."

"Has the Vatican been alerted?"

"Excuse me?"

"Got us a bunch of damn saints from the sound of it."

Harvey frowned at him. "Can't say I care too much for your attitude, mister."

"Harvey, I been studying human nature a long time and one thing I can tell you is there's nobody that squeaky clean. Not even the pope. Now you want to tell me what you ain't you telling me?"

Harvey paused. He started to say something, then stopped himself.

Duggan cocked an eyebrow. "You were going to say something?"

"Well. I probably shouldn't be telling you this."

Duggan waited.

"There was one thing."

"Go on."

"Well...Walt was involved with a woman once. Five or six years ago. Course that's ancient history now." He paused again. "Nobody's perfect, you know."

"I was beginning to wonder."

The men fell silent.

"And of course there was the war."

"Right," said Duggan. "So who was she?"

"Oh. Young gal worked for us. It only lasted a few months. I found about it and Walt promised to end it. We got rid of the gal."

"Got rid of her?"

"We — that is I — fired her."

Duggan nodded.

"Then of course, Marie found out about it. Bound to happen. It was silly to think you could hide something like that in a small town."

"What'd the wife do?"

"Nothing really. They worked through it."

Duggan nodded. "Where's the girl now?"

"Oh." Harvey looked away. "She's a...she passed away."

Duggan cocked an eyebrow. "As in *dead*?"

"That's usually what passed away means."

"How'd she die? And don't tell me it was arsenic poisoning."

"No, no. She did commit suicide, though. But it wasn't poison."

Duggan waited.

"Actually, she hanged herself."

Duggan leaned forward, elbows on his knees, hands in front of his mouth.

Harvey said, "This was years later. She'd moved away. To the city. It had nothing to do with Walt."

"You're positive?"

"Oh yeah. Like I said, it was years later."

Duggan turned that over in his mind.

Harvey stood up and came around the desk. "I think I've told you everything I can. Anything else, you'll have to ask Walt himself." Harvey went over and opened the door and stepped aside.

Duggan stood up. "This girl. She have a name?"

Harvey frowned at Duggan. "Cecilia. Her maiden name was Jennings. Not sure what her married name was."

"So she was married."

"I believe so."

Duggan stuck out his hand. "Okay. I appreciate your talking to me."

Harvey followed Duggan through the showroom to the front doors.

Harvey nodded toward the lot. "That your Pontiac out there, Mr. Duggan?"

"Uh huh."

"What is it, a Fifty-four?"

"That's right."

"Ever think about trading her in on a new model?"

"Every day."

Duggan went out the doors.

Harvey called after him. "Well you know where we are."

"Yeah. That's one thing I do know."

Twenty

It was after three when Duggan pulled up to the sheriff's office. A fiftyish woman with a cast-iron hairdo parked behind the service window told Duggan the sheriff was out on a call. Duggan asked how long the sheriff would be out and she said she couldn't say. He asked if it wouldn't be too much trouble to find out and she asked him if he had an appointment. He said he did, and she said she would be happy to reschedule. Duggan said never mind.

He left the sheriff's office and drove over to the Riverside Motel and checked in. The gaunt old man behind the registration desk said Duggan was lucky, there'd been a cancellation, otherwise they would've been all booked up.

"Really," Duggan said, disinterestedly. "What's going on?"

"Why it's Hobo Days this weekend."

"I don't know what that is," Duggan said, with a yawn.

The old man started to explain, and when Duggan saw it was going to go for a considerable time he cut him off.

"How about the key?"

"Sure. I'll show you to your room."

"That's all right."

The old man insisted. He kept jawing about the Hobo Days all the way to Duggan's room. Duggan wrestled the key from the old man and slammed the door.

He tossed his suitcase on the beat up dresser and tossed his hat on a chair and plopped on the bed on top of the tattered comforter. He propped his head on the thin pillows and picked up the accordion file Ahrens had given him. There was a bundle of letters held together with a rubber band. He set those aside and took out the diary with the broken latch. He studied the date on the first entry. Then he checked the last entry. A fifteen-month time span.

He started reading.

There were entries about new wedge sandals, including illustrations, and details of the family vacation to the Lake of the Ozarks and more than a few awful, sentimental poems. And there was the regulation quantity of teenage angst, not unlike Duggan had felt as a boy:

> I'm not sure what to call what I am feeling right now, but it seems like pure emptiness, the kind where you think you're alone and no one else cares, where you just give up and drift away into deep, peaceful sleep. It feels like melancholy. I suppose this all started when I realized my former crush (now close friend) is telling other girls what he told me, which doesn't make me special at all. I know it's silly to feel this way, but I cannot help it. If only I didn't care about him so. Life would be far less painful. Why, why am I so insecure? If only I were prettier and less plain. But I am kind and I do love to smile and I am trustworthy and I do love to see people happy. People always tell me not to judge a book by its cover, and yet we all do.

Hmm. Duggan yawned and flipped ahead a few pages.

> I've been thinking about others too much and now it's time for me to think about myself for once. My biggest problem is I spend too much time thinking about the past, all the dumb things I've said and done. I need to let go of the past. Tomorrow is another day, right? I must try to remember this. Live in the present!

He'd gotten through about ten percent of the diary when he drifted off to sleep.

It was four thirty when he was awakened by a loud radio in the parking lot. He sat up on the bed, feeling tired and headachy. His stomach rumbled. Coffee might help. Maybe some of that pot roast the chief talked about. He had a couple hours to kill till he could make a surprise visit to the drama teacher. He went into the bathroom and looked at the tub and the large amber roach crawling around the rusty drain. He sniffed his underarms and thought he smelled all right and changed into a fresh shirt and walked across the parking lot.

He'd gone half way across the gravel lot when he spied what looked like a tavern just a little ways beyond the diner. The cracked neon sign said Route 3 Roadhouse. Maybe he wasn't that hungry after all. He turned and headed toward the tavern figuring he could easily kill three hours in a bar.

The tavern was empty save a bartender — a bored, bull-neck in white shirtsleeves — and one old guy with a white billy goat beard and skinny nicotine-stained fingers who sat at the end of the bar under a neon Falstaff light. The joint was quiet too, even though an old jukebox stood by the entrance. Duggan took a seat on a stool and tossed a pack of Winstons on the bar. The bartender came over and stood in front of him but didn't say anything.

"Scotch and water."

The bartender studied Duggan a moment, then he went to the rail and began making the drink. He set the drink down in front of Duggan. "Two bits."

Duggan lit a cigarette and dug into his pants for some change. He tossed back half the Scotch and tried to figure out how he was going to give Ahrens his money's worth. The last thing he wanted was to return any of the retainer.

Duggan tilted his hat back and glanced over at the pale old coot at the end of bar nursing his cigarette and gin. He had all the earmarks of a longtime wino, pallid skin, hooded eyelids, bent posture. His fingernails were long and dirty and he stared through the smoke with unseeing eyes. The bartender slouched over the counter studying the sports page of the *St. Louis Globe Democrat*. He looked like he'd just as soon punch you as talk to you.

At length the bartender snorted and said, "Hear the game last night, Judge?"

The old man in the corner nodded slowly. "I did."

"Played like a bunch of Bush leaguers."

The bartender went back to studying the paper. After a while he said, "Christ. Listen to this." He began reading from the article with all the skill of a fifth grader. "'In the bottom of the seventh Cepeda hammered a line drive down the third base line that skipped through Boyer's legs allowing two runs to score. On the next pitch Cepeda attempted to steal third. Smith's throw to Boyer sailed over the third basemen's head into left field allowing another run to score and giving the Giants a 3-1 ad...advantage.' What a goddamn circus!"

The judge shook his head sadly and blew a torrent of gray smoke from his hairy nostrils. "Going to be a long year," he muttered.

Duggan wondered if the old man was a real judge. No reason you couldn't be both a retired judge and an old wino.

"I'd like to ask you something, if you don't mind," Duggan said to the bartender.

The bartender ignored him.

A moment passed. Duggan pulled out his wallet and set a sawbuck on the bar. The bartender pretended not to notice, but the judge definitely did.

"I'd like to ask you something, if you don't mind,"

Duggan repeated.

The bartender didn't look up. He didn't say anything either.

At length Duggan took out another five and set it beside the ten.

"You can ask me," said the judge.

Duggan turned toward the judge. The old man didn't look at him. "Okay then. You probably heard about that young gal died a few weeks back. The one the paper said was poisoned?"

The bartender's face darkened into a scowl.

"I might have heard something," the judge said.

"Just curious if there was maybe something more to it. Something the paper left out?"

"Curious, eh?" said the judge.

"That's right."

The judge cackled. "You know what they say about curiosity."

Duggan held silent.

The bartender straightened and looked at Duggan. "I don't recollect seeing you in here before."

"My first time."

The judge said, "You from one of them St. Louis newspapers?"

"No. Nothing like that."

"Just curious?" the judge said.

"That's right."

The bartender walked over and stood in front of him. He pushed the two bills back at Duggan.

"Mister I think you're in the wrong bar."

Duggan didn't move. He sized up the bartender, figured he could take him in a fair fight, not that he would expect one. "I was talking to the judge."

"The judge ain't got nothing to say to you. Have you Judge?"

The judge breathed out a cloud of smoke and made no reply.

After a moment Duggan nodded and said, "Yeah, maybe you're right."

He crushed out his cigarette and tossed back the last of the Scotch. Then he picked up the sawbuck and turned and walked out of the bar.

Outside he looked up and down the highway past the diner and the motel and a busy gas station and a few trailers and low-rent houses across the blacktop and wondered where a man could get another drink. Then he remembered the half pint of Jim Beam in his suitcase he'd packed in case of emergency. He strode across the parking lot back to his room. He opened his suitcase and dug around till he found the half pint under his last two clean pair of underwear. He held the bottle up before his eyes. "Should've packed a pint," he muttered. "Oh well."

Duggan carried a chair outside and sat leaning against the doorjamb. He cracked open the half pint and took a long swallow. Then he lit a cigarette and felt around in his pockets till he found the scrap of paper with the list of suspects Ahrens had drawn up for him.

There were five names:

Jackie Hawser
Jerome Todd
Ronny Taylor
Billy Scharf
Ben Miller

Five names. Five suspects. Ahrens had already spoken to the Hawser kid. Duggan had his notes in the file. Not helpful.

Except for the druggist, and the doctors, these were the last people to see Emily Ahrens alive.

The list was probably worthless. When Walt had read the list to him over the phone, Duggan asked again who the most likely suspect was. Ahrens had paused, then said, "Maybe the druggist. Or the Taylor kid."

"That's two. Give me one."

"Taylor."

"Why him?"

"He made the drinks. The last thing she ate or drank. You know?"

"Anything else about him?"

"He's kind of a shitbum."

"Uh huh. That it?"

That was it.

~ ~ ~

Duggan kicked off his shoes and dropped his fedora on the nightstand and lay back on the bed. He thought about strolling over to the diner and grabbing some of that pot roast, but he dozed off instead. When he awoke it was already six-thirty.

He rolled out of bed and walked into the bathroom. A large roach waved its antennae at him from its perch on the faucet. Duggan went back for his shoe and mashed the fucker into a fine pulp, then he combed his hair and splashed some water on his face and drove over to the high school.

He drove around the parking lot till he found the auditorium in the rear of the school and parked the Pontiac by the backstage doors.

The doors were unlocked and Duggan slipped inside.

It took a moment for his eyes to adjust to the dark, so he didn't realize someone was standing beside him staring at him inquisitively.

"May I help you?"

Duggan started and turned to see a tall young woman with short mousey brown hair and thick cat-eye glasses rise out of the gloom.

She looked as plain as a hatrack.

"Yeah. I'm looking for...Shoot." Duggan dug into his shirt pocket and took out the scrap of paper. "Forgot the name of the dude I was looking for." He scanned the list. "Here it is. Jerome Todd."

"Mr. Todd?"

"Yeah. Him."

"May I ask what you want to see him about?"

"It's business."

"Business?"

"That's right."

"Well Mr. Todd is busy."

"We're all busy, Missy."

"My name isn't Missy and tonight is our final dress rehearsal."

"That's nice for you," Duggan said. Then he had a thought. "Say you wouldn't happen to be Mary Pat Scott would you?"

The girl hesitated. "I'm sorry, do I know you?"

"I'd be surprised if you did. Name's Martin Duggan."

She gave him a blank look.

"You are, aren't you?"

"I should be getting back—"

"Yeah, before you rush off though let me ask you something real quick, if you don't mind. Just take a second."

The girl wrinkled up her nose. The man reeked of booze, cigarette smoke and sweaty armpits. "I thought you wanted to speak to Mr. Todd?"

"I do, but..." Duggan smiled in a way that made the girl's skin crawl. "I better explain. You see, I'm a friend of the Ahrenses and they asked me to make a few...whatchamacallits...inquiries...about their daughter."

"Oh," said Mary Pat. She took a slight step back and her eyes darted about the backstage like a small, frightened deer. Sensing she might turn and bolt at any moment, Duggan inched around a step or two, subtly trying to corner her.

"I'm sorry but I don't think I should be talking to you."

"Oh, that's all right, Miss Scott. Like I said, I'm a friend of the Ahrenses."

Mary Pat lowered her eyes and began wringing her hands. "I really don't think I should."

"I understand, but the Ahrenses would really appreciate it."

"I just don't think my parents would approve of...this."

"I completely understand. You're probably still upset about Emma's death."

"Who?"

"Emma. Emma Ahrens."

"You mean Emily?"

"Jesus, you're right. I got a bad way with names. Look, Miss Scott, I know how you feel, I do, but I promised Mr. Ahrens I'd look into this for him."

Mary Pat squirmed.

"I promised I'd try to find out what happened to Emily. It's...it's like this big mystery hanging over everything, you know? Mary Pat — do you mind if I call you Mary Pat?"

"I'd prefer—"

"Imagine how the Ahrenses must feel not knowing what happened to their daughter. I've spoken to them. It's just awful, Mary Pat. Those poor people are tormented."

Mary Pat looked toward the stage. "I really should be getting back."

"Put yourself in their place, Mary Pat. Wouldn't you want to know?"

"Know what?"

"Why what happened to their daughter!"

Mary Pat looked up, her eyes brimming with tears. "Why are you asking me?"

He was beginning to lose her, he could see that. She'd begun trembling all over, but he decided to drive on while he still had her cornered.

"Mary Pat, all the Ahrenses want to know is what happened."

"How would I know?"

"You were Emily's best friend, weren't you?"

"I guess so."

"You knew Emily better than anyone, didn't you?"

"I don't know. Her mother—"

"You were with her the night she died."

"No...I mean, not when she died."

"No. But that evening."

Mary Pat choked back a sob. She took another step back.

"Just tell me what I should tell Emily's family, Mary Pat."

Mary Pat swallowed hard and shook her head. She shuffled her feet.

"Did she ever talk to you about hurting herself?"

"No. Never."

"Was she afraid of anyone?"

"I don't know!"

"Mary Pat, who was she afraid of?"

Mary Pat brushed past him and disappeared behind the curtain.

"Oh for fuck's sake!" Duggan cried, and punched the wall beside him. He put a nice dent in the drywall but his hand was okay.

The curtain parted and a man in his early thirties appeared. He wore a faded tweed jacket with black patches on the elbows and sported a red goatee and shaggy red hair. A beatnik, Duggan assumed.

There were two teenage boys with him. Duggan thought all three looked a little light in the loafers.

"Unless you have school-related business here I'm going to have to ask you to leave," the man said. Duggan was surprised the man's voice wasn't effeminate, but his attempts to intimidate him — if that's what they were — were pathetic.

"You're Mr. Todd, the drama teacher, right?"

"That's right. Now if you don't leave I'll have to call the police."

"Mr. Todd, I'm Martin Duggan and I got a couple of questions I'd like to ask you, if you don't mind." He started to take out his card, but decided not to bother. He glanced around the backstage area. "How's about we step outside?"

The drama teacher looked incredulous. "Perhaps you didn't hear me?"

"Yeah, I heard you all right."

The teacher cocked an eyebrow. "Are you some kind of police officer?"

"A cop? No sir."

"Well, what are you then? What do you want?"

"Like I said, this will just take five minutes, then you can get back to your thing, okay?"

One of the teenage boys turned to the drama teacher. "You want me to telephone the police, Mr. Todd?"

The drama teacher didn't answer. He studied Duggan carefully. "You're not a lawyer. You're a little too seedy looking for that."

Duggan felt like the giving the guy a cuff on the jaw, but he resisted.

"Maybe a reporter." Mr. Todd snapped his fingers. "Yeah. What paper are you with? The *Globe* or the *Post*?"

"The *Globe*," Duggan lied.

"Figures. I read the *Post* myself." Mr. Todd paused. "I don't suppose you're here to do a story on our new production?"

"Well, actually—"

"If you're here about Emily Ahrens I have nothing to say about that."

Duggan scowled. "What is with this town? Everybody has nothing to say about that. At first I didn't think there was anything to this young lady's death. Now I'm starting to think you people are hiding something."

The drama teacher crossed his arms and frowned. "What nonsense. Because we don't want a bunch of strangers poking their noses into our business?"

"Actually—"

"Because we don't want to see our town besmirched in the pages of some big city scandal sheet that knows absolutely nothing about us?"

"Besmirched?"

"Precisely."

Duggan had expected it wouldn't go well. He'd always had a hard time getting people to talk to him, warm up to him. Some PIs had that kind of charming personality or charisma that made people — complete strangers, even — just want to befriend you. Buy you drinks. Tell you anything you wanted to know. Not so with Duggan. People seemed to take an instant dislike to him.

Oh well. No point crying about it.

"Okay, I'm leaving," Duggan said. "But before I go, just tell me one thing. On the night Emily died — and I'll put this to any of you — how did she strike you? Anything about her strike you as odd?"

The teacher glared at Duggan. "You don't give up, do you?"

Duggan shrugged.

"No. Nothing struck me as odd. It was just a normal night. She behaved normally. Everything was normal. Okay? Now if you don't leave immediately I am going to have Billy call the police."

"She wasn't complaining of feeling sick or anything?"

"Billy. Call the police."

One of the boys turned to go.

Duggan said, "Billy? Are you Billy Scharf?"

The boy hesitated.

"Go on, Billy."

Duggan raised his hands. "Okay, okay. I'm going." Duggan glared at the drama teacher and shook his head. "But I sure would like to know what you people are hiding."

Duggan turned and banged out the stage doors. He climbed into the Pontiac and pulled out the scrap of paper from his shirt pocket and studied the list.

"Where to next?" he muttered to himself.

Then he backed the Pontiac out of the parking lot and headed back south toward the drugstore.

Twenty-One

The call came at ten to five. Marie sounded hysterical. Jimmy had come home from baseball practice at four o'clock complaining of a stomachache. Walt smashed down the phone, told Harvey he had to go and ran out the door. He punched the Buick as hard as she'd go and roared fifty miles per hour down the town's residential streets before coming to a screeching halt in the driveway. He slammed the car door and sprinted up the sidewalk and flung open the front door.

Marie looked up, her face pale, her expression grief-stricken. Jimmy lay on the couch in the living room. His hands rested on his belly, his head propped on a pillow. The television showed a cartoon with Daffy Duck and Elmer Fudd.

"Did you call the doctor?"

"Don't you think we should take him to the hospital?" Marie said.

"Sure. But did you call the doctor?"

"No, I didn't think...I—"

"Okay, Walt said, trying to sound calm. He could feel Marie and Jimmy studying him for signs of panic. One little suggestion, he felt, and the whole place might fall apart. He turned to Jimmy. "How you feeling, son?"

"Not so good."

"Stomach hurts, huh?"

"Uh huh. I threw up during baseball practice."

Marie said, "Shouldn't we take him to Children's Hospital?"

"In St. Louis?"

Marie nodded.

"That's too far."

165

"I don't trust St. Mary's," Marie said.

Walt squatted beside the boy. "Let me see your nails."

He could hear Marie muttering a prayer under her breath.

"My nails?"

"Fingernails. Let me see them."

"Why do you want to see my fingernails?"

Walt took the boy's right hand and studied the nails, looking for horizontal lines. He couldn't really tell if there were lines in them or not. The light in the room was bad.

"Let me smell your breath."

"Why?"

Walt leaned in and sniffed. "Breathe," he ordered.

The boy breathed out.

Walt couldn't be sure, but he thought he smelled the telltale garlic smell of arsenic.

"Marie, come here and sniff his breath and tell me what you smell."

"I—"

"Please, Marie," he said sharply.

Marie leaned over her son and sniffed.

"Well?"

"I don't know."

"Anything?"

"What am I supposed to smell?"

"If I tell you you'll imagine you're smelling it."

"Well I don't know. I don't smell anything really."

"Not garlic?"

"Garlic?"

"Yeah. Do you smell it?"

Marie wrung her hands. "I don't know...Maybe."

"Maybe?" Walt snapped. "Dammit, did you or didn't you?"

"I had garlic bread for lunch," Jimmy said.

Walt stared hard at Jimmy. "At school? They gave you

garlic bread?"

"Yeah. We had spaghetti and meatballs and garlic bread."

"Oh for God's sake."

Marie sat on the couch next to Jimmy and took the boy's hand. "Please Walt, we need to go now."

Walt gazed at Jimmy. He looked white as a statue. If nothing else, they'd succeeded in terrifying the boy.

"Okay," he said. "Jimmy, can you walk out to the car?"

"Sure, dad."

Marie grabbed her purse and they walked Jimmy out to the Buick. She climbed into the backseat with Jimmy and he allowed his mother to hold him and press her lips to his forehead while Walt started the Buick. Marie muttered prayers from the backseat and Walt wanted to say that she was just making everyone nervous with her constant praying, but he kept his thoughts to himself.

The drive to St. Louis usually took ninety minutes, depending on traffic. They crossed the Gideon bridge into Missouri past the bronze Boxcar Frank statue that overlooked the Mississippi River and then turned north on Highway 61. They drove most of the way in silence, except every fifteen or twenty minutes when Walt looked in the rearview mirror and asked Jimmy how he was feeling. Outside Ste. Genevieve they pulled over so Jimmy could toss the last of his lunch. After that he lay his head in his mother's lap and she stroked his hair and looked worriedly out the window, her face drawn and white. The drive took longer than usual because of Friday evening traffic and they found themselves stuck repeatedly behind Sunday drivers and tractor trailers Walt was unable to pass.

They rolled into St. Louis just as rush hour thinned out, then immediately ran into more traffic on Grand Boulevard. Walt cursed under his breath and Marie prayed silently and petted Jimmy's head. It was seven o'clock when they pulled up to the emergency entrance of Children's Hospital. Walt left the Buick in front of the emergency entrance and they rushed Jimmy inside.

The emergency room was crowded with anxious parents and noisy, irritable children, mostly whites, but a few coloreds. Walt was surprised and slightly annoyed to see so many Negroes there. He'd figured Children's was a white hospital.

The Ahrenses stood at the registration desk while a country-looking woman in a pattern dress and her dumpy teenage daughter argued with a nurse.

"Them folks just went in there were coloreds!" the woman cried. "You're seeing coloreds before white people now?"

"We'll get to you as soon as we can, Mrs. Cash."

"What kind of place y'all running here?"

"It shouldn't be too much longer."

Walt cut in. "Excuse me."

"I want to talk to your boss," the woman said.

"Excuse me," Walt said. "My son—"

The nurse snapped, "Sir, you'll have to wait your turn." She turned to the woman. "Please have a seat, Mrs. Cash."

"Are we next or ain't we?"

Walt said, "Goddamn it, my son may have been poisoned!"

That seemed to get the nurse's attention. It got Jimmy's attention too. Poisoning was on everyone's minds but it was the first time anyone had mentioned the word outright.

"What kind of poison are we talking about, sir?" the nurse said.

Walt hesitated. He leaned in and lowered his voice. "Well, it could be arsenic."

The nurse looked perplexed. "You're not sure?"

"Well—"

The nurse turned to Marie. Then she looked at Jimmy. "Did you swallow poison?"

Jimmy held his stomach and shrugged.

"Yes or no?"

"I don't know."

"You don't know?"

Jimmy shook his head.

Mrs. Cash turned to the nurse, "Well if he ain't been poisoned he can wait his turn like the rest of us."

The nurse looked at Walt. "What makes you think he might've swallowed arsenic?"

Walt leaned in again. "You see his sister died of arsenic poisoning about two weeks ago."

At that, Mrs. Cash grabbed her daughter by the arm and retreated to the row of chairs.

The nurse said, "Was it intentional?'"

"How do you mean?"

"Did your daughter ingest arsenic on purpose?"

"Oh no," Walt said. He looked at Marie. "She wouldn't have done that."

"So it was an accident?"

Walt frowned at the nurse. "Can't these questions wait till we see a doctor?"

The nurse ignored this. "Did your daughter ingest arsenic accidentally, sir?"

"I don't know. I doubt it."

Marie spoke up, her voice trembling. "We don't really know how it happened. No one was able to tell us."

The nurse studied them silently. At length she said, "So what makes you think your son may have ingested arsenic?"

"Christ!" Walt cried. "Because he's got the same stomachache our daughter had!"

"Sir please lower your voice."

Walt looked up at the ceiling and fought to control

himself. "Sorry."

"Has he been throwing up?"

"Yes," Walt said. "On the way here."

"I threw up at baseball practice too," said Jimmy.

The nurse nodded. "Diarrhea?"

Jimmy lowered his eyes and nodded.

"Headache?"

"A little, I guess."

"Burning sensation in your throat?"

"Uh, not really."

The nurse wrote something down. "How do you feel now?"

Jimmy shrugged. "My stomach hurts a little."

"Is it a sharp pain or more like a dull pain?"

"Dull, I guess."

Walt leaned in. "Miss, please. Can you get a doctor to look at him? We drove all the way from—"

"Have a seat and I'll give this information to the nurse."

"Nurse? Goddamn it, we need to see a doctor!"

"Sir, I'm going to ask you to please calm down."

Marie took Walt's arm. "It's okay, honey."

Walt glared at the woman, but he allowed himself to be led away. Marie brought him to a row of orange chairs on the far side of the waiting room. Jimmy followed.

Once seated, Walt turned to Jimmy. "How you feel, boy?"

Jimmy shrugged. "A little better."

Walt sighed. "Feel like you've got to throw up?"

"Not right now."

Walt nodded and rested the back of his head against the wall and stared blankly out over the waiting room.

A nurse came out and called the name of Wanda Cash, and Mrs. Cash and her daughter stood up. The woman muttered "Finally!" and they followed the nurse through a pair of swinging doors.

"Squeaky wheel gets the grease," Walt said.

Marie leaned towards Walt and patted his hand.

"We should've gone to St. Mary's," Walt muttered.

Marie looked at the floor. "I'm sorry."

They waited another five minutes before a nurse appeared and asked them to follow her. They were taken to a room curtained off from many other rooms. Walt spied the Cash women in one of the rooms as they walked by. The nurse flung back a curtain and said, "Have a seat. A doctor will be with you in a minute."

She flung the curtain closed.

"Jesus Pete," Walt said. "I thought this was an emergency room. It's no different than a goddamn doctor's office."

They sat down on three flimsy looking chairs, Jimmy between them. Jimmy looked at his mother.

"Mom, am I going to be all right?"

Marie took Jimmy's hand in hers. "Yes, honey. You're going to be fine. These are the best doctors anywhere. They'll take good care of you."

"Promise?"

"I promise."

Walt stood up and began pacing around the little curtained area. "If there isn't a doctor here in three minutes I'm going to raise some Cain."

"Walt, sit here with us," Marie said, patting the empty chair beside her. Walt looked at his wife and softened. He sat down beside her and nervously tapped his foot on the floor.

Another five minutes passed before the curtain swooshed back and a young man wearing a lab coat and striped tie stepped in. He thrust his hand toward Walt. Walt grunted to his feet and shook the doctor's hand.

"I'm Dr. Hamilton." He looked at Jimmy. "Understand

you've got a tummy ache, young man."

Jimmy nodded.

"How's about hopping up on this table for me?"

Jimmy climbed up on the table. The doctor lifted Jimmy's eyelids and peered in his ears and up his nose and down his throat. He asked Jimmy to lie back on the table and he pressed on the boy's stomach. "Does this hurt?"

"A little."

"How about this?"

"Uh huh."

The doctor nodded. "How long has your stomach been hurting?"

"Since history class."

"And what time is history class?"

"It starts at one o'clock."

The doctor asked Jimmy a few more questions and poked and prodded some more. Then he turned to Walt. "The nurse said you were concerned he might've ingested a toxic substance?"

"That's correct."

"What makes you think that?"

Walt turned the doctor aside and whispered, "You see two weeks ago his sister died of arsenic poisoning."

The doctor stared at Walt, surprised. "Arsenic?"

"Yes."

"How did she...how was she exposed to it?"

"We don't know."

"You don't know?"

Walt shook his head.

"Was there an investigation?"

"Yes, yes," Walt said shortly. "It was useless. Nobody could tell us anything. I've had to hire a private investigator."

"Hmmm." The doctor turned back to Jimmy. He studied his fingernails and smelled his breath.

"He had garlic bread for lunch," said Walt.

The doctor looked at Jimmy. "You did?"

"Uh huh."

"And that's all you've had to eat today?"

"Since breakfast. I had Corn Flakes."

The doctor nodded and turned to Walt and Marie and said he'd be right back.

Walt grumbled and sat down next to Marie. She patted his thigh.

Jimmy said, "Can I get down now?"

"Not yet, honey."

At length Dr. Hamilton reappeared, this time with a much older man sporting a crop of fine white hair and very thick spectacles.

"This is Dr. Timmons."

Dr. Timmons pretty much went through the same questions and pokings and proddings as Dr. Hamilton. Then the two doctors excused themselves and stepped outside of the curtained area where they could be heard talking in low tones. Walt heard Dr. Hamilton thank the older doctor who then walked off. The curtain whooshed back and Dr. Hamilton stepped inside.

"Well, it's nothing serious, you'll be glad to know," he said.

"Oh thank God!" Marie cried.

"Then what is it?" said Walt.

"Most likely he's got a stomach bug."

"A bug?"

The doctor turned to Marie. "Is he allergic to any medications?"

"No," said Marie.

"Wait," Walt said. "Like a virus? Like the flu?"

"Correct. There's a lot of that going around this time of year. Especially in the schools. Spreads like gangbusters."

Walt was incredulous. "Are you saying he's got the

flu?"

"That's correct."

"Walt," Marie said, resting her hand on his arm.

"Hold on, Marie," Walt said, getting to his feet. "That's the same thing the doctors said about his sister. That it was a stomach bug. And two hours later she..." He pulled the doctor aside and lowered his voice. "And two hours later she was dead."

"Walt," Marie said.

"I understand that, Mr. Ahrens."

"You hardly examined him! And now you're saying it's just a bug!"

"I assure you, Mr. Ahrens, viral gastroenteritis is nothing to sneeze at. It can be very painful. It can even be fatal if untreated."

Walt glared at the doctor and folded his arms over his chest. "Well we'd like a second opinion."

The doctor frowned at Walt. "Mr. Ahrens, we just got a second opinion. That's why I called in Dr. Timmons. He's a toxicology specialist. One of the best. Now I'm going to—"

Walt turned to Marie and Jimmy. "Let's go!"

"Walt, please," Marie said.

"We're going to St. Mary's. Where we should've gone in the first place."

"That's you're prerogative," said the doctor.

"Damn right, it is. Let's go."

Walt threw back the curtain and stormed down the hall toward the exit. Marie, a pained look on her face, mouthed the words "sorry" to the doctor.

Dr. Hamilton nodded. "I understand, Mrs. Ahrens. Best thing for Jimmy is to drink a lot of water and get some rest. If he's hungry give him toast, bananas, bland things." He smiled and touched her arm. "I expect he'll be fine in a day or two."

"I'm sure you're right—"

"Marie!" Walt's voice echoed from the corridor.

Marie gave the doctor a weak smile. "Come Jimmy," she said.

Jimmy hopped down from the table and followed his mother down the corridor toward the front entrance.

On the way to the Buick, Walt said, "We're going to St. Mary's."

"Please Walt, can't we just go home?" said Marie.

Walt stared at her disbelievingly. "I can't believe you'd say that, Marie. After everything we've been through."

"Walt, I trust these doctors."

"Doctors," he scoffed.

"Please, Walt?"

Walt stared at her for a long minute, then he turned to Jimmy.

"How you feeling, Jim?"

Jimmy shrugged. "Better, I guess."

The sun slanted low above the surrounding buildings. Walt pressed his lips tightly and gazed off across the parking lot at the rows of cars reflecting the red and purple hues of sunset. Suddenly he felt very tired. It was like someone had opened a spigot and all his energy had drained away.

"Okay. But if you start feeling bad we're going to St. Mary's, and that's final."

Marie smiled wanly.

On the way home they took a small detour and drove past Sportsman's Park where the Cards were playing the Pirates. They rolled down the windows and turned on the car radio and listened to the play by play on KMOX. From the Buick you could hear the roar of the crowd and smell the aroma of roasted peanuts and red hots. It was a fine, familiar smell.

It smelled like life.

Twenty-Two

Officer Joe Waddell slumped at the counter of the soda fountain. The clock on the wall showed just after eight o'clock. Outside a hard gray rain drummed on the roof of the drugstore and pocked the street. Waddell slurped on a chocolate soda and gazed around the empty drugstore.

"Rescheduled for tomorrow morning."

Ben Miller nodded without looking up.

"Ten o'clock."

The druggist sat on a stool behind the counter going over a thin pile of receipts and entering numbers into a ledger. He stood up and stretched and took off his lab coat. Then he rolled up his sleeves and went back to the receipts.

The police officer selected a toothpick from the chrome dispenser and set about working on his teeth. He gazed at the boarded up front window, then back at the druggist.

"First time they ever had to cancel it, that I can recall."

Ben scratched some numbers into his ledger.

The police officer yawned and regarded Ben.

"Chief says a truck threw a rock through your window."

"That's correct."

"Some freak accident."

"Uh huh."

"So you didn't see it?"

"I didn't see it."

The cop nodded and suctioned up the last of the chocolate soda.

"Say, there's something I been meaning to ask you.

How come you fired my cousin Ronny?"

Ben looked up from the ledger and scowled. The cop was on his second free chocolate soda.

"Look around you," Ben said, motioning toward the empty store. "How can I afford help when I have no business?"

Waddell dropped the used toothpick in an ashtray. "Yeah, but firing Ronny's only going to make things worse."

"Worse it could not get."

Waddell studied the druggist, his face propped in both hands. "You sure talk funny. All backwards like. Is that a Jew thing?"

"A Jew thing? Yes. It's a Jew thing."

The shopkeeper's bells above the door tinkled and an unfamiliar middle-aged man entered, shaking the rain off his fedora. He peered squinty-eyed around the dark, empty store. Ben studied the man, but couldn't quite place him. He looked vaguely seedy and citified. The stranger walked over and sat on the stool two down from the police officer.

"Coming down good, ain't it?" said Waddell.

"Good for the crops," said the stranger.

"That it is," said Waddell. "You a farmer?"

"Me? No. Why, do I look like a farmer?"

"Not a bit."

The stranger wasn't quite sure what to say to that, so he turned to the druggist. "How's the coffee?"

"We're out. I could make some fresh."

"That's fine," said the stranger.

Waddell belched and regarded the stranger. "You look familiar. Are you a Schmidt?"

"Not me."

Waddell nodded and studied the stranger more intently. "Huh. I could've swore you was a Schmidt."

The stranger dropped his Stetson fedora on the counter. "Nope. I ain't from around here. Name's Duggan."

"Well, Mr. Duggan, welcome to Gideon. Here for Hobo Days, I expect?"

"Actually I'm here on business."

"Business, huh? What kind of business you in, if you don't mind my asking?" The cop held up his hand. "Wait, let me guess." He eyed him closely. "Shoe salesman?"

"Nope."

"No?" He snapped his fingers. "Farm implements."

Duggan shook his head.

"I got it. Crop insurance."

"I wish. Probably make a hell of a lot more money."

Waddell laughed. "Wouldn't we all."

Duggan moved his hat out of the way and leaned on his arms on the counter. "I'm in the private investigative industry."

"Yeah?" Waddell looked puzzled by that. He pushed his empty glass across the counter, hoping for a refill, and turned back to Duggan. "So, how you like it so far?"

"How do I like what?"

"The town."

"Oh." Duggan glanced around the drugstore and shrugged. "Kind of quiet."

Waddell chuckled. "Well, that's because every one's out at the picnic grounds."

"Kind of wet for a picnic."

"Yeah. They had to cancel the parade this evening. First time that's ever happened."

"That's too bad," Duggan said disinterestedly.

"Where'd you say you was from?"

"East St. Louis."

"Yeah? I got a cousin lives there. You know a Terry Waddell? Works over at the Armour meat packing plant."

"I don't think so."

"Big guy. Red head. Missing most of his left ear?"

Duggan shook his head.

"Yeah. Kind of a big town, I guess, East St. Louis."

Duggan glanced at a plastic-coated menu that listed about fifteen different sodas and several flavors of ice cream.

Ben got the coffee going and drifted back to where the two men were seated. A wind gust slammed a sheet of rain against the plywood window. Ben looked at Duggan. "Get you anything else?"

"No thanks." Duggan set down the menu. "You're Ben Miller, right?"

Ben looked up. "That's right."

"Might I have a word with you?"

"Actually pharmacy hours are over."

"It ain't about that."

The cop leaned in intently.

"Only take a minute of your time."

Ben cocked an eyebrow. "Is this a sales call?"

"No, nothing like that."

"I'm sorry, who did you say you are?"

"His name's Duggan. He's from East St. Louis," the cop said.

Duggan took out his wallet and handed Ben the same dog-eared business card. Ben studied the card, turned it over, and started to slide it into his shirt pocket.

"Mind if I have that back?"

"Oh...Sure."

Duggan replaced the card in his wallet. "I represent Warren Ahrens."

Waddell said, "You mean Walt Ahrens?"

"Yeah. The car dealer."

"I used to work for him," said Waddell.

Duggan ignored this.

"So Walt done hired him a private dick," Waddell said.

"If this is about the death of Mr. Ahren's daughter I don't have anything else to say on that matter," Ben said.

Duggan lifted his hands defensively. "Hey, I understand completely. You want to put it behind you. Trust me, Mr. Ahrens wants to put it behind him too."

Waddell said, "That ain't what I hear."

"All I need's a couple minutes of your time."

Ben scowled and closed the ledger and placed it under the counter. "Like I said, I've said all I care to say on the subject." The druggist turned to the police officer. "Officer, will you escort this man from the premises?"

Waddell lifted his eyebrows, but didn't make to get up.

Duggan said, "Okay, Mr. Miller, I'll make this quick. Just tell me why you fired that boy, Ronny Taylor."

"That's what I want to know too," said the cop.

Ben shot Waddell an angry look. "I've already told you why."

The cop turned to Duggan. "He said it was on account of business being bad. If you ask me firing Ronny only made business worse."

Ben flared. "Nobody asked you."

The cop turned back to Duggan. "The boy's all tore up about it. Heck, everybody knows he didn't have nothing to do with that girl being dead. What was it she died of again?"

"Arsenic," said Duggan.

"Yeah."

Ben squared himself and crossed his arms.

Duggan looked at the cop. "So what do you think happened?"

Waddell said, "Well now, the chief thinks it was a suicide and I reckon he knows better than anybody."

Ben came out from behind the counter. "I'm going to go ahead and close up now. If you two gentlemen don't mind."

"Eight thirty on a Friday night?" Waddell said.

"That's right."

"What about the man's coffee?"

"Try the diner. It's open till midnight."

Waddell looked at Duggan and shrugged. "I was about to head over there anyway."

Duggan slid off the stool and turned to the druggist. "Look, Mr. Miller. Just answer me one more thing. Was there anyone in the store that night you didn't know? Strangers, I mean? Out-of-towners?"

Ben walked over to the sign on the door and flipped it around to CLOSED. He opened the front door. Rain sprayed through wetting his shoes.

"Have a good night, Mr. Duggan. Officer."

Waddell slid off his stool and hitched up his trousers and shuffled toward the door. "Thanks for the sodas," he said.

Duggan walked alongside the police officer. "People sure are tight-lipped in this town."

"Could be they just don't like strangers."

"Could be," Duggan said. "Say, where can I find this cousin of yours?"

"Which cousin?"

"Ronny Taylor."

"Oh. Probably at the fairgrounds." He gazed out the door at the rain sheeting down. "Actually, with this weather, maybe not. You might find him at the roadhouse."

"That's that dive out on Route 3?"

"That's the one. Look for a blue T-Bird. But he probably won't talk to you neither."

Ben stared down at the floor as the two men walked out into the dark rain. Then he quickly closed the door and slid the deadbolt into place.

He turned out the front lights and for a long while he stood in the dark storefront listening to the sound of the rain drumming against the windows and the occasional low rumble of distant thunder drifting over the river. He stood a long time, till the desire to smash every goddamn thing in the store past.

Twenty-Three

Duggan drove straight to the roadhouse and pulled into the lot and found a parking space near the front door. Sure enough a light blue T-Bird sat gleaming under a yellow vapor light on the north side of the bar.

The place appeared to have picked up considerably since Duggan left. The parking lot was three-quarters full, pickups mostly, but a few campers too. Probably tourists in town for that dumb-ass hobo thing. Inside, the bar was murky and thick with tobacco smoke and echoed with the pleasant click of pool balls, drunken laughter and Wanda Jackson on the jukebox.

Heads turned to stare as Duggan entered. A few of the clientele were dressed like bums, or hobos, rather. There looked to be only one guy in the bar under twenty-five, a kid with a pompadour wearing a white T-shirt with a pack of cigs rolled up in the sleeve and skin-tight denim jeans who circled the pool table. The kid strutted around languidly, like he'd seen too many Marlon Brando movies, and stopped to chat to the waitress. Duggan took a seat at a table near the pool table and waited for the waitress to notice him.

She took her sweet old time about it.

"What can I get you?"

"Beer."

"Any special kind or ain't you particular?"

He lit a cigarette and snapped the Zippo shut. "As long as it's wet."

"One Stag, coming up."

"Say, you know a kid named Ronny Taylor?"

She stared hard at Duggan. "Why do you ask?"

"No reason. That him you were just talking to?"

"I'll get your beer."

"I'll take that as a yes."

The waitress gathered up some empties and went over to the bar and whispered something to the bartender who looked over at Duggan with a sour look. Duggan half expected the bartender to come after him with a baseball bat.

At length the waitress brought his Stag and a glass that looked like it hadn't been washed since the Roosevelt Administration. Teddy Roosevelt. Duggan picked up the bottle and left the glass on the table and strode over to the pool table. He set a quarter on the edge of the table and leaned against a silver radiator and gulped his beer, watching the match and hoping the Taylor kid came out on top so maybe the opponent — a dude dressed in a patchy coat, a dusty bowler hat and shoes with the toes sticking through — would get lost so they could talk.

For once Duggan got lucky. On the next shot the hobo knocked in the eight ball.

"Goddamn, twice in a row," he said and turned to Duggan. "Guess you're up, pal."

The hobo tossed his cue on the table and stalked off toward a cluster of other hobos. Duggan picked up the cue and a piece of chalk and rubbed some chalk over the tip while the kid racked the balls.

"Your break," he said.

"What're we playing?"

"Eight ball ain't good enough for you?"

"Just asking."

Duggan broke, leaving the kid four or five easy shots. He sunk three of them. When his turn came Duggan played terrible, like he'd never seen a pool table before. Neither one said much for the first five minutes. Then the kid began feeling cocky.

"Don't think I've seen you in here before."

"First time."

"Yeah? Here for the picnic?"

"No, why do you ask?"

"I figured the way you was dressed."

Duggan shot and missed.

"Actually, I'm here on business."

"Yeah? Let me guess. Shoe salesman."

"Nope. Nothing like that."

The kid called the six ball in the corner pocket and sunk it.

"Coal?"

Duggan shook his head.

"Them's the only business we got, except the prison."

Duggan said, "Actually I'm working for a guy named Ahrens."

"Yeah? The car guy?"

"That's right."

"That dude sold me my T-Bird."

"That's yours, huh? Nice."

"You sell cars?"

"Nope. Actually I'm in the private investigative industry."

The kid stiffened.

"I'm looking into the death of Mr. Ahrens' daughter."

The kid locked eyes with Duggan. "Say, what is this?"

"Eight ball. And I'm getting my ass kicked."

"Mister I ain't even started."

Duggan grinned. The kid was wiry, but scrawny like a chicken neck. Duggan could snap him like a dry twig if need be.

"My name's Marty Duggan."

"Well Marty, I got nothing to say to you."

Duggan laughed. "That don't surprise me. Whole town is like a goddamn Trappist monastery."

The kid looked at Duggan. "I don't know what that is."

Duggan started to explain, but the kid cut him off. "Does Ahrens really think I had something to do with his daughter?"

"Did you?"

"Fuck no."

"Okay then."

The kid shook his head. "Why is it anytime something bad happens in this town people think I done it."

Duggan shrugged. "You tell me."

The kid lined up a shot, but decided against it.

"You don't strike me as such a bad kid," Duggan said.

The kid frowned, like he'd just been insulted. "Did you talk to the druggist, Miller?"

"Tried to. He wasn't much of a talker either. I asked him why he fired you."

The kid leaned on his cue. "Yeah? What'd he say?"

"He told some cop it was on account of business being slow."

"Slow? He wishes business was just slow. He ain't had more than six customers since that girl died."

"Yeah? Why's that?"

"Because that chick was at the drugstore a couple hours before she died."

Duggan nodded.

"Died of fucking poison."

Duggan drained his beer and set the empty on the edge on a nearby table. "So people think she got poisoned at the drugstore?"

"Some do," he said with a shrug. "People are idiots. Miller wasn't even there that night. He'd already gone home by the time she showed up. The people in this fucking town, they're just chickenshits. And some just don't like Jews. They say Jews been poisoning Christians for thousands of years." The kid lowered his voice and nodded across the bar. "See that dude over there by the cigarette machine."

Duggan looked toward a gaunt man wearing the blue-gray duds of a coalminer.

"The other night he was in here trying to stir up lynch mob. To go after Miller."

"Yeah?"

The kid straightened. "He was serious, too. Course he's a crazy motherfucker so nobody listened to him. All them coalminers are. Comes from being in the dark all day, I guess."

Duggan nodded thoughtfully.

"I'm fucking pissed at Miller, but I don't want to see him getting his ass lynched."

Duggan nodded and stared down at the table. "What am I, stripes or solids?"

"The way you play, you don't have to worry about it."

Duggan laughed and banked the nine ball into the side pocket. "I believe I'm stripes."

The kid killed off his bottle of beer and belched. "Worse part is I'm going to have to try to get on at the mines now. I hate the fucking mines. Gave my granddaddy and grandma black lung."

"Your grandmother worked in the mines?"

"No. But she washed my granddaddy's clothes every day. That'll do it." The kid stared at Duggan a moment. "You ain't from around here are you?"

"East St. Louis."

"Really? You know Chuck Berry?"

"No. I don't go in for that hillbilly crap."

The kid shrugged and nailed three shots in a row.

Duggan watched in silence and took another pull off his bottle. At length he said, "How about you? It must've been rough for you. You served her that night, didn't you?"

The kid drew out a pack of Lucky Strikes and shook one from the pack. "You ask too many questions."

"Occupational hazard."

The kid glared at Duggan. After a while he said, "Yeah, I served her that night. So what? I served a lot of people." He looked away. "You want to know what I think? I think she killed herself. Plain and simple."

"Why would she do that?"

"How the hell would I know? Dames are screwy."

Duggan nodded. "What'd you mean when you said you get blamed for everything bad that happens?"

The kid shrugged. "You never stop, do you?"

Duggan knew better than to respond to that.

"I ain't ashamed of what I done. So I hotwired some jalopy? And me and some cats took it for a joyride. Took a curve too fast and turned over."

"Ouch."

"Got me two years in juvie."

Duggan nodded.

The kid laughed. "Turned out it was the mayor's wife's coupe. How's that for luck?"

"So you don't think Miller had anything to do with her death?"

"Shit, that square? I can tell you this, whatever happened didn't happen at Miller Drug."

"No? The timeline fits."

The kid sank the two ball and strode smugly around the table, chalking his cue. He turned to Duggan and said, "I'm going to put you out of your misery right now."

Duggan leaned on his cue, watching. "Did you know her? Emily Ahrens?"

The kid set up his shot. "Naw. I mean, I knew who she was. But I didn't *know* her. Too square for my tastes."

He knocked in the four ball. That left the eight.

"I'm curious. Does Miller sell arsenic?"

"Shit man, I don't know. Who knows what he's got back there behind the counter? I wasn't allowed anywhere near the pharmacy."

Duggan nodded. "Right. Dumb question."

The kid sunk the eight ball.

Duggan looked on appreciatively. "You ain't half bad."

"Damn straight. That'll be a five spot."

"We were playing for five bucks?"

"Hell yeah."

Duggan scowled and dropped the cue on the table and pulled out his wallet and handed over a five spot.

"Nice doing business with you," the kid said, pocketing the money. He glanced around the bar. "Who's next?"

Duggan folded up his wallet and shoved it in his back pocket. He drained his bottle and turned and started for the door.

It was easy to see why Miller fired the little dirtbag. What he couldn't understand is why he ever hired him in the first place.

Twenty-Four

Walt stared at the alarm clock on the nightstand beside his bed. The face glowed toxic green in the gloom showing quarter to one. Beside him Marie snored deeply under the influence of Dr. Fischer's sedatives. He sat up and felt with his feet till his toes found his slippers, then he lifted himself quietly off the bed and slipped into his terrycloth robe and shuffled down the hallway. He paused outside Jimmy's room. From inside came the crackle of a transistor radio broadcasting a ballgame. When a Cardinals game ended Jimmy would scroll up and down the dial till he found a Kansas City or Detroit or Chicago station, before drifting off to sleep to the play by play of some distant American League game. Down the hallway Gary the cat sat outside Emily's bedroom door, his green eyes like saucers in the dark. Walt went on down the hall. At the bottom of the stairs he turned and strode into the kitchen. He stood a while looking out the open window above the sink at the distant porch lights, his mind moving in a dozen directions. Far across town echoed the long low blast of an air horn from a Union Pacific locomotive. He opened the refrigerator and found a bottle of beer and he leaned against the counter and drank half the bottle in a single swallow. He pulled the chain on the light over the sink and opened a drawer full of junk Marie had collected, Green Stamp books and coupons, a few cookbooks and old church envelopes. He closed the drawer and began going through the cabinets. Dishes, cups, mugs, wine glasses. He moved on down the row. The next one contained canned goods. He lingered there and studied the contents. Green Giant green beans. Van Camps pork and beans. Campbell's cream of chicken soup. Lima beans. Great Northern Beans.

Marie loved her beans.

Another cabinet held flour, sugar, cornstarch, salt, oatmeal, syrup, vegetable oil, cake mix. He opened the cake mix bag and peered inside. He'd spent his lunch hour at the city library, in the reference section. He started with the encyclopedia, studied the entry for arsenic, then moved on to the chemistry section, which proved too technical for him. Apparently white arsenic could resemble flour. Or sugar. Salt too, probably. Walt took down the bag of C&H sugar and peered inside and wet his finger and dipped it into the bag.

He held his finger to his tongue.

It was sugar, all right.

He jammed his thumb a bit further down into the bag and tried another sample.

Definitely sugar.

He located the saltshaker on the countertop and unscrewed the lid and shook some grains into his hand. Too much. He dumped all but a few grains into the sink and tasted the crystals.

Salty.

He discarded the rest into the sink and screwed the top back on the shaker. He looked into the cabinet and took down a bag of Gold Medal flour and opened the bag and peered inside.

What the hell did flour taste like anyway?

Walt sighed. The whole thing was idiotic. What was he expecting to find? That somebody, somehow planted arsenic in their bag of sugar?

He set the bag down and opened another cabinet and peered inside. He took down a box of stick matches. Cake pans and muffin tins rattled. He pushed a pan aside and the stack slid and clattered to the countertop. Walt cursed angrily and sent the rest of the cake pans and tins crashing to the counter, then he let out a cry and swept them all to the floor.

He folded to the kitchen floor and sat leaning against the bottom cabinets, his fists bunched in his hair and hot tears scorching his face.

"Dad?"

Jimmy stood wide-eyed in the kitchen doorway, Emily's cat tucked in his arms. He wore his cotton baseball pajama pants and a gray T-shirt.

"Are you okay?"

Walt wiped his face with his sleeve. "Sorry. Guess I woke you."

"I wasn't sleeping."

Walt shook his head and got slowly to his feet. "I thought I'd make a little midnight snack and I...I got all tangled up in these stupid pans."

Jimmy didn't say anything.

Walt began picking up the trays and pans and stacked them on the countertop.

He looked at Jimmy. "How's the tummy?"

"Better."

"That's good. Want to join me for a snack? Your belly's probably empty as a church on Monday morning."

Jimmy laughed. He set Gary on the floor and the cat bolted toward the stairs.

"Sure."

"That a boy."

Walt opened the breadbasket and took out a loaf of Wonder Bread.

"Here we go."

He took down some more jars from the cabinet. "How about a PBJ and a glass of milk?"

"Sure."

"You want to get the milk and glasses?"

"Okay."

Jimmy got the bottle of milk from the still crammed

icebox and picked out two glasses from the dish strainer and carefully poured the milk while Walt went to work on the sandwiches. He carried the glasses to the kitchen table and pulled up a chair.

"Crust on or off?" said Walt.

"On's fine."

"On it is."

Walt cut the sandwiches diagonally and placed them on small sandwich plates and carried them over to the table and sat down across from Jimmy.

"Dig in."

Walt always felt a little awkward when he was alone with his son. He could talk to strangers — car customers in particular — all day long, but around Jimmy he felt self-conscious and ill at ease. It was hard to say why. Perhaps it had something to do with his relationship with his own father. Walt had always felt awkward and anxious around his father. He now wondered if his dad had felt the same. They'd had very little in common, even after Walt had grown. Walt liked sports and movies and his dad thought such things were trivial and childish, a waste of time and money. About the only thing his dad liked were cars. He always seemed to be buying a new one, often when the family could least afford one.

It now occurred to Walt that going into the car business might've been his way of gaining his father's approval.

He never did though. His father died a month before Walt and Harvey Gilster opened their car dealership.

If nothing else, Walt and Jimmy had sports in common. They could talk about baseball and football, even hockey, till the cows came home. Thank God. Walt always said sports was the language of men. Without sports there would be only the sound of female voices.

"Find any good games tonight?" said Walt.

"Tigers and the Indians. Tigers won by six."

"Who was on the mound for Detroit?"

"Bunning."

"Well no wonder."

They finished their sandwiches in silence.

At length Jimmy said, "How long do you think Gary's going to sit in front of Emily's door like that? It really makes me sad."

"I know," Walt said. "Why don't you take him into your room?"

"I tried, but he won't stay. He goes over to my door and cries till I let him out, then he goes right back to Emily's door."

Walt turned toward the kitchen window, studying the dark reflection of him and his boy at the table. Walt shook his head. "It's hard. On all of us. Even Gary."

He turned back to Jimmy. "So, you're holding up all right?"

Jimmy swallowed a mouthful of milk. "I guess. The worst times are when I forget she's gone and I start to go over to her room to ask her help on some math problem or something and I see Gary and the door closed."

"Yeah."

"I get this big old lump in the pit of my stomach."

Walt reached out and rubbed the boy's shoulder. "I know. I get the same feeling. Maybe...maybe with time it won't hurt so much."

"I hope so," Jimmy said. He set down his glass. "I miss her, dad."

"Course you do. We all miss her."

Jimmy gazed at the half eaten sandwich in front of him. "Dad, are we going to be all right?"

"Of course we are, Jim. Why do you ask?"

"It don't seem like it."

Walt thought about that. "Are you talking about going

to the hospital today?"

"You think someone's trying to hurt us?"

"No. Gosh no, Jim."

"Then why'd you hire that man?"

Walt paused. "Oh. You know about that?"

Jimmy nodded.

"Well. I just...I just want to figure out what happened to your sister, that's all. I know it won't change anything, but I sure would like to know. You know? I thought maybe this man could find out for us. Find out what happened."

Jimmy stared silently at his sandwich.

"You want me to let it go, don't you?" Walt said. "You and your mother both want me to let it go."

Jimmy shrugged.

Walt stood up. He picked up their dishes and glasses and carried them to the sink. "I wish I could, Jim. I really wish I could."

"Why can't you?"

"It's hard to explain." He shook his head. "But I feel like I owe it to your sister. To try."

Jimmy stared at his father, trying to work it out in his mind. "What if nothing happened? What if she done it to herself?"

Walt locked eyes with his son. "She wouldn't have done that. Never."

Jimmy looked away.

Walt sat down and stared hard at the boy. "Jim, do you know something you aren't telling me?"

Jimmy shook his head.

Walt grabbed Jimmy by the arm and shook him roughly. "Do you? Jim?"

Jimmy took in a sharp, audible breath and the skin on his neck crawled.

"What do you know?"

"Nothing!" Jimmy shrieked and shot up, knocking

over his chair. He glared angrily at his father.

Walt colored violently, his voice catching in his throat. "Jesus, Jim, I'm sorry."

Jimmy turned and ran from the kitchen.

Walt made a fist and thumped himself in the forehead. "Jesus. I got to get it together before I lose my goddamn mind."

Something rubbed against his leg and Walt started. Emily's cat fixed her wide green eyes on him.

"Walt?" Marie's voice drifted down the stairs. "Honey, what's going on doing down there?"

"Nothing, Marie. Go back to bed."

He picked up the chair and pushed it under the table. Then he looked around the kitchen one more time before turning off the light.

Twenty-Five

Duggan woke to a loud rapping on the door. Somehow the knocking seemed mixed up with the dream he was having.

In the dream he was banging the cocktail waitress from the roadhouse when they were interrupted by a man's voice. "I know you're in there!" he hollered.

"My husband!" the waitress cried.

This was the way all of Duggan's sex dreams ended, with somebody trying to kill him. A psychoanalyst would've a field day with Duggan.

The knocking started up again.

"Housekeeping!"

Duggan blinked his eyes open and tried to remember where he was.

Oh yeah.

He groaned and rolled over in bed and fumbled around the end table for his wristwatch, knocking over a tumbler of water. He found his watch and dried it off on the oily bed sheet and checked to see if the watch still worked.

It did. It was quarter after eleven.

Duggan rolled onto his back. A fresh wave of pain washed over him, nailing him to the bed. The worst of it seemed centered right behind his eyes and radiated out from there, endless tendrils of sheer agony. He swallowed and his throat felt raw and sore. This was no hangover. He was coming down with something. A summer cold, probably. The worst kind.

His system wasn't used to all this fresh, manure-tainted air.

More pounding.

"Yeah!" Duggan cried hoarsely. "I'm coming!"

He wrapped himself in the thin dingy sheet and shuffled toward the door, shivering like an over-caffeinated Chihuahua. Chills, great. He cracked the door and peered out. An elderly woman, her face a ridiculous mass of deep lines and crevices, squinted up at him. Her thin, brittle gray hair sat uncombed and matted atop her derelict face and a stub of cigarette dangled from her thin, formless lips. The cleaning woman.

"You think you could come back a little later?"

"You want me to come back?" she croaked in a voice ruined by ten thousand cigarettes.

Duggan turned his head and sneezed. A loud, wet, doubled-over sneeze. "Could you? That would be wonderful."

The old woman eyed him coolly. "Check out time is eleven."

"Just ten minutes."

"We weren't sure if you was checking out today or not."

Duggan wasn't either. The thought of being back home, recuperating in his own filthy but familiar bed had a definite appeal. He adjusted the sheet over his chest. The old woman scowled at the unorthodox use of her linens and blew a puff of smoke out the side of her mouth.

Dammit, he'd had a feeling this case would be a stinker. He could probably hang around this shithole another six months and still not learn a damn thing. Maybe a better detective than he could find out something, someone with more smarts, more charisma, more empathy for the common folk. Duggan had no illusions about his gifts as an investigator. This case only served to remind him how unexceptional he was.

Unless it was a missing person's case or a bail jumper. Give him one of those to work and he'd sniff him or her out in a week or less. Ask him to tail some cheating spouse or repossess a car and he'd be all over that. But this. What the hell was this anyway?

Whatever it was, the cops didn't want to touch it. And the rubes didn't want to talk about it.

And what was up with this Ahrens guy, anyway? Duggan was starting to get the feeling there was something not right about him.

Well?" the old woman snapped.

Duggan looked up.

"Are you checking out or not?"

"I'm thinking."

"Well, don't take all day about it."

"Let me ask you something. Do you know a Walt Ahrens?"

"Who?"

"Ahrens. Walt."

"You mean that feller owns the car dealership?"

"Yeah. You know anything about him?"

"Why would I?"

"I just thought, you know, this being a small town."

The woman glared at him.

Duggan sneezed again and wiped his nose on the sheet.

The woman scowled. "Mister this pail's getting heavy. You want the room or not?"

Duggan shivered again. "Reckon I'll mosey along."

"That's fine. We can use the room. It's our busiest weekend of the year."

"I know. Hobo Days. Give me ten minutes."

The old woman muttered something and shuffled on to the next unit.

Duggan slammed the door and glanced around the room. At least he hadn't unpacked. Mostly because he didn't want bedbugs or roaches or whatever it was lurked in those drawers stowing away in his clothing.

The thought of leaving town seemed to have a medicinal effect on him. On his mood anyway.

"Well, can't win them all," Duggan muttered to himself, and shuffled into the bathroom to fetch his toiletries. He blew his nose on some toilet paper and picked up the plastic cup with his toothbrush in it and a roach the size of a candy bar scrambled up over the lid onto his hand. Duggan started and dropped the cup. The toothbrush splashed down in the toilet and the roach landed on this foot. Duggan cursed and squished the bug. He felt his skin crawl. Goddamn place was filthier than his office. He fished his toothbrush out of the toilet and studied it. Then he dropped it in the waste can. Another negative in the old expense column.

He slipped into the same suit coat and paints and shirt he'd worn the day before — what the hell, he wasn't trying to impress anyone, not anymore. While he was at it, he lifted the clothes out of the suitcase and made sure no roaches had taken up residence. Then he slammed the suitcase shut and gave the room the once-over.

He turned off the lamp and slammed the door and strode toward the motel office. The same old-timer slouched behind the registration desk studying a St. Louis newspaper. He glanced up from the paper. "Howdy."

"Checking out."

"Already, huh?"

"That's right."

The old man set aside the newspaper and stood up creakily. He slipped on a pair of reading glasses and peered into the registration book. "Get over to the Hobo Days, did you?"

"Huh? Uh no. But there's always next year."

"Sure, bring your young ones next time."

Duggan sneezed.

"Gesundheit!" the old man said. "Summer cold?"

"Uh huh."

"Them's the worst kind. Let's see now, that comes to fifteen fifty, plus tax."

Duggan peeled off a ten, a five and a single, but before he handed them over he said, "You wouldn't happen to know a guy named Walt Ahrens?"

"Terrance? No. Can't say as I do." He reached for the cash, but Duggan held back.

"Ahrens. Owns the big car lot in town."

"Oh, him. Sure."

"Thinking of buying a car over there. Is he a good man to deal with?"

"Couldn't say."

"No?"

"Nope.

"Guess you bought your car elsewhere."

"That's right."

Duggan handed the cash to the old man, who studied the bills closely, then bent over and slipped them into the drawer under the counter.

"Too bad you ain't feeling well. The municipal band's playing over at the Rotary Club pavilion tonight."

The old man turned and squinted at a brochure rack on the counter. He selected a brochure and ticked off half that night's scheduled events before he turned back and found himself looking at his bucket-toting wife.

"Talking to yourself again, you old fool?" she snapped.

"Hmm. There was a young man here a minute ago," he said.

The old woman eyed him skeptically.

"Well, there was," he muttered quietly before going back to his newspaper.

Twenty-Six

The couple from Red Bud had returned and stood looking over the same '57 Coronet. The young man eased in behind the wheel, a large grin on his face like he was imagining himself with a scantily clad Sophia Loren at his side.

"Had time to think about it?" Walt said, walking up.

"Some."

"Almost sold her yesterday. This old boy from Du Quoin came in looking for something sporty. Models like this don't usually stay around this long. Yes sir, you sure are lucky there."

Walt glanced up and watched as Duggan's Pontiac pulled onto the lot. He wasn't expecting the private eye and he felt a sudden tightening of his bowels. Maybe he'd found something. Why else would he come by without calling first?

Hell, maybe the case was solved.

The Pontiac stopped by the front doors and Duggan eased out slowly and stiffly like a man in serious pain.

The young man climbed out of the driver's seat and said, "I think maybe—"

Walt cut him off. "Folks, I need to talk to this gentleman a moment. My partner will be with you in just a sec."

The young woman fumed and elbowed her husband. "Say something!" she hissed. Her husband opened his mouth and began to speak, but Walt had already walked off.

He strode up to Duggan and extended his hand. The private eye looked a little rough this morning. Worse than before. Rumpled suit, unshaven, bloodshot eyes. Who cares? As long as he had good news.

"Let me get my partner to help those young folks and we'll go in my office and talk," Walt said. He didn't wait for Duggan to respond.

He found Harvey on the telephone.

Duggan followed Walt into Harvey's office. He leaned against the door jam and blew his nose into a crusty handkerchief.

Harvey looked up at Walt and held up a finger. "But we had the space reserved six months ago," he spoke irritably into the phone.

Walt sighed. Besides being picnic chairman, Harvey was in charge of the model plane show at the Breezy Hill Complex that afternoon. There must have been some sort of conflict. Walt stood by and tapped his foot anxiously.

Harvey said, "Who did?"

Walt pointed out the window toward the young couple. The young man now leaned against the Coronet and seemed to be arguing with his wife.

"Well that's not my problem," Harvey told the caller.

Walt picked up a pencil and a piece of scratch paper off Harvey's desk and scribbled: "Young couple very interested in '59 Coronet." He underlined the word "very" twice. He handed the note to Harvey, who studied it briefly, but didn't respond.

"Who told him that?" Harvey said.

Walt turned and almost ran into Duggan. "Sorry. Let's go into my office."

Duggan nodded.

A voice came from the showroom. "Excuse me! Hello!" It sounded like the young man from Red Bud.

Walt shouted down the corridor, "My partner will be out in just a sec. That's a great little car there!"

He led Duggan down the corridor to his office and closed the door. "Have a seat. Would you like some coffee?

It's fresh."

"No, that's all right. I think I got a cold."

"Summer colds are the worst."

"Uh huh."

Walt dropped down behind his desk and took off his glasses and rubbed his eyes. He looked at Duggan expectantly. "So, you got some news for me?"

Duggan shifted uncomfortably in his seat and swallowed gingerly. "Well. You see, Wally—"

"Walt."

"Oh right. Sorry." He paused. "You don't happen to have any aspirin, do you, Walt?"

"No. I don't think so."

Duggan nodded. "No, I guess not."

Walt leaned forward anxiously. "So?"

"Yeah, so I done a little investigating."

"More than a little, I hope," Walt said followed by a short, nervous laugh.

Duggan removed a notepad from his jacket pocket and wiped a finger beneath his nose and flipped through a few pages. "So, I talked to a number of people."

"Uh huh."

"I talked to the druggist."

"Ben Miller."

"Yeah, Miller."

"What'd he have to say?"

"Not much. Nothing useful."

Walt frowned at him. "Yeah."

"And I talked to Mary Pat Scott."

"That's good. I wasn't able to talk to her."

"Yeah. I know." Duggan paused. He could feel a sneeze coming on, but he fought it. "She wasn't very helpful either."

"Really?"

"I also talked to the chief." He looked down at the pad.

"Stokes."

"A.W."

"Yeah. And the drama teacher."

Walt tightened his lips and nodded thoughtfully. "And?"

"And I talked to Ronny Taylor."

"Yeah? What'd that little shit have to say?"

Duggan looked up. "Well, one thing he said is he gets blamed for everything bad that happens in this town."

"Probably with good reason."

"He also said some guy was talking about lynching the druggist."

"Yeah?" Walt laughed. "When was that?"

"Last week. Didn't go through with it though, obviously."

"No. I expect I would've heard about that." He chuckled. "What else?"

"He said he didn't know your daughter."

Walt frowned at Duggan. "That's a goddamn lie. She was at that drugstore pretty much every weekend."

Duggan shrugged.

"What else?"

"Well, he said I asked too many questions."

"Little shit," Walt said. "And?"

"And that's about it."

"That's it?"

Duggan snapped the notepad shut and slipped it back into his jacket pocket.

"You see Walt, the fact is—"

Someone knocked on the door and Harvey poked his head inside. "Excuse me. Walt, I don't see that young couple out there."

Walt turned and glanced out his window. "Hmmm. They must have gone."

"Gone?"

"Appears so."

Harvey scowled.

The room fell silent.

"Okay then," Harvey said, and closed the door. A little too forcefully, Walt thought.

"Sorry about that. You were saying?"

"Yeah. Walt, the thing is—"

The telephone on Walt's desk began ringing.

"Go on," Walt said.

The phone rang again.

"Well, I—"

The phone rang a third time.

"You can get that," said Duggan.

"That's okay. My partner will get it." Walt got up from his desk and walked over and opened the door and yelled out into the hallway. "Harv, can you get that?"

The phone continued to ring.

"Harv?" he shouted down the corridor.

"I really don't mind."

"Damn it, he was just here a second ago. Why the hell doesn't he pick up?" He walked a few paces down the hallway. "Harv?"

Duggan reached across the desk and picked up the phone. "Hello, Ahrens and Gilster Automotive."

A woman's voice said, "Who is this?"

"Martin Duggan."

"Is this Ahrens and Gilster?"

"Yes ma'am. How can I help you?"

"Well," she said hesitantly. "Is Walt there?"

Walt wandered back into the office.

Duggan held the phone up to his chest and whispered. "It's for you. A dame."

Walt scowled. "Is it my wife?"

Duggan shrugged.

"Tell her I'm busy. Say I'm with a customer."

Duggan held the phone away from him and sneezed loudly. He set the phone on the desk and blew his nose into his handkerchief and picked up the phone. "Mr. Ahrens is with a customer. Can I take a message?"

There was a short pause. "Who is this again?" the lady said.

"Martin Duggan."

"Oh. Well, no, that's all right. I'll ring him back a little later."

"That's fine, ma'am," Duggan said, in his best hick voice. "You have a nice day, you hear?"

Duggan hung up the phone.

"Who was it? My wife?"

"She didn't say."

Walt nodded. "Anyway, you were saying?"

Duggan sighed. "Well, it's like this, Walt. I read the coroner's report, the transcripts from the inquest, the diary, the letters. I talked to a shitload of people."

"And..."

Duggan shrugged. "And I don't know."

Walt stared in disbelief. "You don't know?"

"I don't know."

"What the hell's that supposed to mean?"

"Look Walt. I'm going to put down everything on paper for you, but the fact is I didn't learn a damn thing we didn't already know."

"Nothing?"

"Nothing useful. I mean, I learned that the Taylor kid stole a car once."

"Hell everyone knows that."

"That's what I mean. It's a small town. Everything that happens here is general knowledge. You can't fart without everyone hearing about it. I'm sniffing around here trying to dig up information everybody already knows. Has known for fifty years. Except me. And nobody's going to tell me anything because I'm an outsider."

Walt sat back in his chair and his tone softened. "Well hell, Marty, you just started. You've only been at it a couple of days. Give it some more time."

Duggan shook his head. "More time ain't going to help, Walt. Not in this town. Besides, I need to get back. I got some unfinished business I need to take care of."

Walt waved his hand dismissively. "To hell with that. Hell with the facts then. What do you *think* happened? Who do you suspect? That's what I want to know."

"Who do I suspect?"

"Yes, for Christ's sake. Who do you think did it?"

"You mean who did I think poisoned your daughter?"

"Yes, dammit! You must suspect someone. Everybody in this goddamn town suspects somebody. Including me!"

"Who suspects you?"

"People. You think I don't hear things?"

"Why would they suspect you, Walt?"

"That's what happens in these kind of cases. Suspicion falls on family members. Jeez, you're a private eye. You don't know this?"

Duggan sniffed.

"A wife or a daughter dies, the husband, the father, he's the prime suspect." Walt stared at Duggan. "I thought you used to be a cop?"

"Yeah, sure Walt. Hell, I know that. I just never heard it about..." Duggan frowned for a second, calculating. "Well, if it's any consolation I don't suspect you."

"That's great. So are you going to tell me?"

"Tell you?"

"Who you suspect?"

Duggan shifted uneasily in his chair. He glanced out the window across the parking lot. A teenager in a high school letterman's jacket was taking a soapy sponge and a garden hose to the wood paneled station wagons on the east side of the lot.

"Look Marty, I paid you good money. Don't tell me it was for nothing."

Duggan stared across the desk at Walt. The retainer was gone. If he had to refund any part of it he'd be in the hole. And he was already in the hole from a gambling debt. Big time.

Think, Marty, think.

"Okay. For my money there's only one person who could've done it."

"Now you're talking. Who?"

"The soda clerk."

Walt paused. "Ronny Taylor?"

"Yeah."

"That's who you suspect?"

Duggan nodded, trying to look confident.

Walt thought this over. "Not Miller?"

Duggan thought, Dammit. I should've said Miller.

Duggan shook his head. "Definitely the soda clerk."

"Ronny Taylor." Walt turned this new information over in his mind. "You know, I had my suspicions about that little sonofabitch. He's got a reputation in this town as a troublemaker."

Duggan took out his handkerchief and blew his nose raucously. "So I hear."

"Stole a car a few years ago and wrecked it. Did a bit of time for that, I believe."

Duggan slipped his notepad into his jacket pocket.

Walt continued. "A real delinquent." He stared off, thinking. "So what makes you suspect *him*?"

Duggan swallowed hard. "Well, the way I figure, he was the only one with the opportunity."

Walt nodded. "That's true."

"We talked to just about everyone who was with your daughter that night and the only thing she had to eat or drink after dinner was an ice cream soda served by you-know-who."

"Yeah, but—"

"And God knows it's easy enough to get arsenic. The shit's laying around every barn in the county. So the question is, why'd he do it?"

Walt nodded.

"We know he's capable of grand theft auto. Which is a very serious offense."

Walt leaned forward. "Uh huh."

"Then Miller fires him. What's that tell you? Miller knows something, but he ain't talking."

"You talked to Miller, you said."

"Yeah, but he clammed up. The whole goddamn town is like a mess of clams."

Walt furrowed his brow. "But you haven't told me why Taylor would want to poison my daughter? What's his...what do you call it? His motive?"

"I know. And if I was a cop I'd bring that little runt in and work him over with a rubber hose till I got the answer."

"Then why don't you?"

"Because I ain't a cop. And you ain't paying me enough that I'm going to get thrown in the Greene County Jail for assaulting a local resident."

Walt thought that over. "So how much would it cost?"

"Forget it, Walt. Not interested."

Walt paused. "So you're sure it was the Taylor kid?"

Duggan nodded. "I'd bet my bottom dollar on it."

Walt stared down at his desk. After a while he glanced up at Duggan. "So what do we do?"

"That's up to you, pal. The cops ain't going to do a damn thing, I can tell you that."

"So what then?"

Duggan shrugged. "Look Walt, I've done all I can here.

Like I said, if I was a local cop I think I could get the kid to talk. But I ain't."

Walt stared silently down at his desk.

"You related to any of these cops? Seems like everybody's related to everybody else around here."

Walt shook his head. "No. Nobody that would do that."

"Too bad," Duggan said, standing up. "As for my charges, I think we're about even. But I'll send you my report and an itemized bill next week."

Walt nodded absently.

Duggan turned to go, then halted at the door. "I'm real sorry about your daughter, Walt."

Walt didn't say anything.

Duggan turned and walked out of the office and down the corridor to the showroom. He nodded across the lot to Harvey Gilster, who nodded back, then he eased into the Pontiac. His headache seemed to melt away as he started the engine and drove off the lot.

He kept the Pontiac under thirty-five till he reached the town limits, then he floored it the rest of the way home.

Twenty-Seven

Walt uncovered the footlocker under the stairs behind some boxes of old sports magazines. Beneath some bundles of letters, photographs and postcards, he found his Colt service pistol. He hadn't fired the pistol in a good ten years, but then he didn't intend to fire it tonight either.

He hoped not, anyway.

He checked the cylinder. The Colt wasn't loaded.

He tugged his shirt out of his pants and slipped the Colt into his waistband and climbed back upstairs. He stood in the doorway to the living room and looked in at his wife and son, both half asleep in front of the television, and said, "Going out for a bit." Before Marie could question him he slipped out the front door.

Walt pointed the Buick south. He'd start at the roadhouse out on Route 3. If the T-Bird wasn't there he'd drive the streets and backroads till he found it. There weren't that many T-Birds in Gideon and even fewer blue ones.

He cruised past the roadhouse. Sure enough, the T-Bird sat under a lone vapor light in the north corner of the lot, away from the pickups and junkers where its doors wouldn't get dinged by careless drunks. He whipped the Buick into the lot and pulled in next to a Chevy pickup with a cracked windshield and a banged up fender. He shut off the engine and rolled down the driver's side window and lit a Lucky Strike while he thought over his next move. He didn't really have a plan. Just a wild hair based on what Duggan said about making the kid talk.

He turned on the radio keeping the volume low and listened to the last inning of the baseball game. Presently an old man, who looked like the pale ghost of Judge

Saxton, hobbled out of the bar and folded into a Cadillac Coupe de Ville. Damned if it wasn't the judge. How the mighty had fallen. The judge sat behind the wheel a long while till Walt guessed he must've passed out, then he started the Caddy and jerked it into reverse, slamming into a pickup behind him and doing some serious damage to its grille. The judge sat there a moment, gathering his wits, then he jammed the Cadillac into drive and pulled out onto the highway. In fits and starts the Cadillac rolled off toward town.

The game ended and Walt turned off the radio. In the silence the muffled twang of country music oozed from the cinderblock walls of the bar. A kid like Ronny Taylor, he could very well close the bar down.

Walt flicked away his butt and opened the glove box and fished around till he found his old Swiss Army knife. He slipped the Colt from his waistband and put it in the glove box and then he eased out of the Buick. If there were anybody in one of parked vehicles, couples necking for instance, he couldn't see them. No telltale red dots of cigarettes. And if they were screwing in the backseat they probably wouldn't notice him anyway.

He strode nonchalantly toward the T-Bird and dropped down beside the rear driver's side tire and rapidly plunged the blade into the sidewall. The tire flattened like a cheap accordion. He stood up slowly and gazed around the lot. The lights of a passing tractor-trailer washed over him briefly, then darkness returned and all was quiet save the whine of the semi and the muted music from the bar. He crawled up to the front tire and sunk the blade to the hilt. The tire hissed and collapsed. He got up and walked casually back to the Buick and eased in behind the wheel. He held his wristwatch up to the dashboard light and checked the time. Eleven o'clock.

Some time passed before a rusted GMC pickup pulled

into the lot. The truck parked next to the Buick and Walt scooted down in the seat and turned his face away. A young dude in a leather jacket and shitkicker boots climbed out and strode toward the bar, walking right past the T-Bird without noticing the flat tires.

Walt settled back into his seat. Might as well get comfortable. It was going to be a long night.

Twenty-Eight

He was jolted awake by the sound of a powerful engine stirring to life and loud rock and roll music. Walt sat up and gazed out the front windshield. The lot was mostly empty now, but an overhead light illuminated the inside of the T-Bird. The kid was alone. He must not have seen the flat tires. The car jerked and pulled out of the lot, the deflated tires throwing up gravel. Walt started up the Buick and pulled out of the lot, keeping a good deal of distance between them.

The T-Bird wheeled and fishtailed onto the highway at high speed. The car had traveled a good tenth of a mile before it slowed, then jerked off to the shoulder in a cloud of white dust. Walt slowed the Buick.

A moment later the kid tumbled out of the T-Bird and walked up to the front of the car. He gazed drunkenly at the flat, then curse loudly and reared back and kicked at the tire. He staggered and caught himself before he could fall.

Then he saw the flat rear tire.

"Fuck!" he screamed, and kicked at the rear tire.

This time he toppled over and fell on his ass in the rocks.

Walt pulled up behind the T-Bird. He kept the engine and headlines on.

The kid muttered a few curses and brushed off his hands and slowly crawled to his feet.

"Car trouble?" Walt called through the driver's side window.

"Fuck! Two flat tires! Goddamn it!" Ronny glanced up into the Buick's headlights. He held up a hand to shield his eyes from the glare. "I know the sonofabitch who done this too."

Walt swallowed hard. He reached over and slid the Colt from the glove box and slipped it into his jacket pocket. Then he eased out of the car and slowly walked up the shoulder. The highway was empty of other vehicles.

"You're Ronny Taylor, right?"

Ronny looked up and recognized Walt. "Oh, hey, Mr. Ahrens. Didn't know it was you. Sorry about the language."

"That's all right. Wow, bad luck, huh?"

Ronny laughed mirthlessly.

Walt said, "Do you have a spare?"

"I sure as heck ain't got two spares."

"No, I guess not." Walt studied the tires a moment, then he said, "Climb in. I'll give you a lift."

"Thanks, but no way am I leaving my T-Bird on the side of the highway."

"No worries. I'll call a tow truck after I drop you off. Where would you like it towed?"

Ronny leaned against the car door and thought this over. "Gee. I don't know. Towing's going to cost a fortune."

"Tell you what," Walt said. "I sold you this vehicle. I'll tow it to our shop for free. Got a couple of used tires I could give you too. How's that for service?"

Ronny stared at Walt. "Wow, thanks, Mr. Ahrens."

"No problem. Come on, climb in."

Ronny shuffled over to the Buick and eased into the passenger seat. Walt started the engine and pulled the Buick back onto the highway.

"Where to?"

"Home, I guess."

"Where's home?"

"Blackburn Lane."

Walt nodded. "Just got to make one pit stop first, if that's all right."

"You're driving." A darkness filled Ronny's eyes. "I'm going to get that son of a gun."

"Who?"

"Frank Boetcher. I know it was him."

Walt knew Boetcher. Vaguely. A local good-for-nothing shitbum. He'd had to repossess his pickup a year ago.

"How you know it was him?"

Ronny laughed. "I was being friendly with his girlfriend, if you know what I mean."

"Ah."

Ronny pumped his fist into his hand. "Nobody messes with my T-Bird."

They drove north past dark fields of soybeans and alfalfa and the occasional ruined red barn and jutting grain silo and turned off the highway onto a secondary blacktop and drove for a while in moonlit stillness. Walt tuned the radio to WSM and they listened to the country station. Ronny sank down in his seat, his head bobbing up and down, muttering drunkenly about payback. His eyelids drooped and his chin dropped to his chest. Walt steered the Buick carefully down the highway and turned onto a gravel road that wove through long stretches of timber, whipping past dark trees and dodging the occasional ghostly white possum. The Buick's tires crunched along for a while then the car splashed through a narrow rocky creek and the road turned to rutted dirt.

Ronny sat up and glanced out the window from time to time. At length he turned to Walt. "Dang, where we going, Mr. Ahrens?"

"Just a bit further."

"Looks like we're out in the boonies."

"Almost there."

The Buick crept on a few more yards till the road dead-ended at a stand of pine. Walt put the car in park and turned off the headlights.

He calmly reached over and popped open the glove box and fished around till he found a metal flashlight. Then he pushed open the passenger side door. The overhead light blinked on.

"Get out, Ronny."

Ronny turned to look at Walt, puzzled.

"Huh?"

"Out. Now."

"What the heck's going on, Mr. Ahrens?"

"Go on."

"Seriously, what the heck is this?"

Walt pulled the pistol from his waistband and held it so Ronny could get a good look at it.

"I said get the fuck out."

Ronny seemed to sober up instantly.

"Jesus, Mr. Ahrens. What the hell did I do? I didn't do nothing."

Walt jammed the Colt into Ronny's ribs and the kid yelped and slid off the seat and out the door of the Buick. His feet hit the ruts and he lost his balance and tumbled into some weeds and bushes, cursing angrily. Walt eased out the driver's side door and walked around the Buick. He turned on the flashlight and cast the light around him in a broad semi-circle till he located the kid on the ground. Ronny's eyes widened and locked on the Colt. He climbed awkwardly to his feet and held his hands out in front of him and took a few steps backward toward the trees and brush.

"Take it easy, man. I don't know what you think I did, but I didn't do nothing."

Walt clutched the flashlight with one hand and wielded the Colt with the other. He pointed the flashlight behind Ronny. "That way," he said, trying to make his voice firm.

"Okay, just take it easy with that." Ronny turned and took a few tentative steps in the darkness. The tree cover had choked out the moonlight and the darkness was absolute.

The wind picked up and hushed through the leaves. The smell of sap thickened. All around them limbs groaned in the breeze.

Walt kept the light and the Colt trained between Ronny's shoulder blades. All at once the forest floor became a carpet of pine needles which muffled their footsteps. They went on, single file, for some fifty yards, then Walt halted.

"That's far enough."

Ronny froze. He couldn't see Walt's face, or anything else for that matter, just the ray of flashlight as it washed over him.

"This is about your daughter, ain't it, Mr. Ahrens?"

Walt sweated profusely, but remained silent.

"I tell you I didn't have nothing to do with it. I swear! You got to believe me!"

Ronny took a step back and tripped and fell on his ass. He began scuttling backward on his hands and heels through the needles.

"If somebody said I had something to do with it, he's a goddamn liar."

"Do with what?"

"Nothing. I didn't have nothing to do with anything. I told you. I just worked there."

Ronny ran up against a tree trunk and stopped. He held out his hand, trying to shield his eyes from the light.

"Come on, man. I swear, I never hurt no one! This is crazy!"

"You're a regular angel, is that it?"

Ronny was beginning to blubber now and choked on his snot and tears.

"Didn't you just tell me you were going to kill Frank Boetcher?"

"It was a joke. Jesus! It was just talk!"

"You going to tell me you didn't steal Jed Gershenson's car?"

"That was four years ago! I was just a kid!"

"Okay, Ronny. Here's how this works. You don't leave here till you tell me what happened to my daughter. Or you don't leave at all."

"Christ, Mr. Ahrens, I just told you, I don't know. Shit!"

Walt raised the Colt and stepped toward the kid, slowly, deliberately. He tried to get to his feet, but Walt kicked his feet from under him and he dropped back to the ground. He lay on his side and looked up at Walt.

"Fuck man!" he cried. "What do you want me to say? I swear I didn't do nothing to your daughter. I didn't even know her! Why would I want to hurt her?"

"You tell me, tough guy."

Ronny slowly got to get to his knees. He put his hands out in front of him. "Jesus, what do you want from me?"

Walt shone the flashlight in his eyes. "I want to hear you say you poisoned my little girl."

"What?"

"You heard me."

"Are you fucking crazy? I ain't saying that!"

"I'm going to blow your goddamn head off either way, so you may as well get it off your conscience."

Ronny's head drooped and hot tears stung his eyes. He felt his bladder let go. He began sobbing. "Goddamn it, Mr. Ahrens, I didn't do anything."

Walt moved closer, rested the muzzle against Ronny's forehead. "Then who did?"

"I don't know," he cried. "I mean, I thought she killed herself."

"That's a goddamn lie!"

Ronny turned his head, cringing. Walt jammed the muzzle into his ear.

"I'm done messing with you, son. You had your chance to confess."

Walt pulled back the hammer with his thumb. The hammer clicked into place.

Ronny cupped his hands to his face. "Okay!" he cried. "All right. I'll tell you. Just put the gun down. Fuck!"

Walt held the Colt level and stared hard at the kid, his eyes narrowed to folded slits. Goddamn, he thought. It worked. Duggan was right. The kid *was* going to talk.

"I'm listening."

"Okay," Ronny said. "Just put the gun down."

"I'm going to put this Colt up your ass if you don't start talking."

"All right. Jesus." Ronny leaned an arm down and started to get to his feet, slowly, his hands covering the wet spot at his crotch. "Okay," he said, and lashed out with his hand, knocking the flashlight out of Walt's grasp.

The flashlight spun away into the darkness and the beam extinguished like a blown-out matchstick.

Walt dove after the flashlight but the ground seemed to fall away and he landed hard on his shoulder. He got on all fours, feeling along the needles at the sticky, pine tar earth and rough cones and fallen branches, but it wasn't there. From nearby came the sound of footfalls crashing through underbrush growing fainter.

"Sonofabitch!"

To hell with the flashlight. Walt scrambled to his feet and started blindly in the direction of the footfalls. He hadn't gone five steps when he was clotheslined by a low-hanging branch. His feet flew up in front of him and he landed hard on his ass. He sat up and shook his head, dazed among the pine needles, a mouse rising on his forehead and blood trickling around his eyebrows and down his cheeks. He'd dropped the Colt when he fell and now he got to his knees, feeling blindly through the needles, first left, then right, till his fingers found the warm steel of the barrel.

He held still and listened. The crackle of brush was fainter still. He got to his feet and moved on, more cautiously this time, his free hand outstretched, feeling his way in the dark. Sweat soaked though his shirt and stung his eyes.

Might as well be a goddamn blind man.

A foot caught on a fallen log or something and he stumbled again, but managed to catch himself. His hearing came up: the drone of locusts and the long muffled hoot of a barred owl, which sounded like "Who cooks for you? Who cooks for you all?"

Nothing else.

He'd lost him.

Goddamn it, the sonofabitch had been about to confess too!

A yellow pair of lights floated high in the trees, brights from a vehicle rolling down HH Road, followed by a low distant hum. Walt halted, wiped the sweat from his eyes.

A sound startled him, like the crash of a body slamming through bushes and Walt set off again in blind pursuit, following the crack of snapping branches. The kid was heading toward the vehicle, toward the roadway. Walt limped on in ragged pursuit. The blacktop lay just a hundred yards or so ahead. The oncoming vehicle droned louder.

The kid leaped from the trees, clambered down a narrow embankment and onto the blacktop. Walt made out his silhouette in the approaching headlights, his arms waving frantically at the approaching pickup. The truck came on steadily, picking up speed on the downhill slope.

At the last minute the kid lunged out of the way, but the driver swerved and met him side-on with an incredibly loud thud. The kid was flung upward onto the hood and slammed against the windshield. He spun off and thumped under the rear wheels like an old rag doll. The tires locked—bald rubber skidding and squealing—and the pickup spun one-eighty before coming to a dead stop.

The radiator hissed a geyser of steam and the engine clanged softly. Walt could just make out the murmur of a Sam Cooke song.

"Darlin' yooooou send me."

One truck headlight dangled loose like a dislocated eye. The other shone into the woods, glinting off Walt's Colt. For a moment Walt seemed frozen in the beam of thick clear frost. Then he found his footing, and backed up slowly, one step at a time, before he turned and sunk back into the darkness.

Twenty-Nine

The pickup jolted to a stop.

Roger's breath came short and hard and his heart drummed as if he'd run a great distance.

The truck's one good headlight was trained on the side of the road, washing over a wall of timber that ran along the highway. Roger blinked through the blood-smeared spiderwebbed windshield.

"What the hell?"

He closed his eyes and looked again.

He was gone.

Roger craned his neck down the blacktop road.

Darkness.

A strong pain in his right knee announced itself. He unbuckled his seatbelt and hobbled out of the truck, favoring his right leg. The night was cool in the hills. He took a few steps, then turned back and leaned inside the truck and reached behind the seat for a toolbox and removed the flashlight.

On the radio Webb Pierce started singing a song about the Tupelo County Jail.

He found the kid some twenty yards back, sprawled by the side of the asphalt road, curled on his side. His breath came shallow and ragged.

"Christ Jesus," Roger murmured. He knew the kid. It was the Taylor boy, from the drugstore.

"What the hell were you doing out here?"

Roger squatted beside the kid, searched and found a weak pulse. Christ, the kid's blood was everywhere. It drained from his mouth and nose and pooled around his head. His eyes were rough slits.

"Just hang on, pal."

Roger turned and his gaze followed the headlight back to the treeline. A cloudy swirl of insects danced in the beam. The engine idled and ticked. Webb Pierce finished his song and a commercial came on. "Ahrens and Gilster Auto Sales...The new 1960 models are in...Go see Walt and Harvey..."

Roger turned back and the kid was still, his eyes like empty glass marbles. He felt for a pulse and couldn't find one.

He'd just come out of nowhere. Out of the trees like a goddamn deer. Like someone had been chasing him.

He'd thought it was a deer, too, for a split second. Till he saw the kid's bewildered face smack the windshield, the look of sheer horror and disbelief in his eyes.

At most he'd been driving five miles over the limit. They could gauge it from the skid marks, the troopers could. He'd been groggy. It was late. But no way was any of this his fault.

Roger turned back to the kid and slowly got to his feet. He was going to have to move him. Though moving him would surely kill him. If he wasn't already dead.

Roger limped back to the truck and prayed the engine would start.

He reached in and turned the key.

It turned right over.

He backed the truck within a few feet of the kid. He thought it best to lay him in the bed, even though it didn't seem right, dumping him back there like a buck he'd taken during bow season.

He laid his sleeping bag in the bed and moved his fishing poles and tackle boxes aside. There was no good way to do this. Nothing to use for a stretcher and no time to fashion one.

The kid didn't look like he weighed much. One forty, maybe. Roger squatted, groaned and lifted the kid under his arms and walked him to the tailgate, feet dragging, and laid him down. He climbed into the bed and hauled the kid along the bed and laid him down on the bag. The kid hadn't made a sound.

Roger hopped down from the bed and fetched a blanket from behind the seats and covered him and tucked it under so it wouldn't blow away.

Not that it mattered. The kid was gone anyway. He didn't even bother to check his pulse again.

Roger gazed back toward the pines one last time and slammed the tailgate. The gate failed to catch and dropped with a crash. He slammed the gate again. This time it held.

Yes sir. Like someone had been chasing him.

Thirty

Roger limped down the corridor to the nurses' station. His denim shirt and canvas fishing jacket was soaked with the Taylor's boy's blood from trying to wrestle him into the bed of the pickup. His hands were washed, but the rest of him...he could've been mistaken for a hog butcher.

"Hey Barbara. There a phone I can use?"

The nurse looked up, her eyes wide. "Jesus, Roger, what happened?"

"Long story."

The nurse pursed her lips and nodded toward the phone in the station. "You can use ours."

"It's kind of private. Is there another phone?"

"There's a payphone downstairs. By the front entrance."

"Thanks."

He took the elevator to the first floor. Some peckerwood was on the phone, arguing loudly with someone. From the sound of it, he was going to be a while. Roger strode through the front doors and stood on the sidewalk in front of the hospital and zipped up his canvas jacket. A roiling sea of dark clouds skidded slowly across the slate-colored sky. He watched a state trooper's patrol car turn into the lot and pull up to the emergency entrance. The trooper climbed out of the vehicle and went through the doors to the emergency room. Roger didn't recognize the man.

What had the kid said?

"I didn't do nothing?"

Roger glanced back through the doors. The phone was free. Roger stepped inside and fished some coins from his pocket and dialed Walt's number. Marie picked up on the third ring. She sounded groggy.

"Hey Marie, it's Roger. Sorry to call this time of night."

"Roger?" She said. "Is something wrong?"

"Well, actually—"

"Is it Walt? Is he okay?"

"Actually, Marie, I was calling to speak to Walt," he said. "So he's not there?"

"No. He had to go out." She paused, relief creeping into her voice. "So he's okay?"

"I don't know. I mean, I assume he's fine."

"Oh." Marie paused. "I thought when you called..." She paused again. "Why did you want to speak to Walt?"

"It can wait till morning, Marie. I'm sorry I woke you."

"I was awake," she said. "It's very late, isn't it?"

"I'm sure he'll be home any time now."

Marie nodded silently.

"Well, good night, Marie."

Roger hung up the phone and turned and almost collided with the state trooper.

"Mr. Tully?"

"That's right."

"Mind if I ask you a few questions?"

Roger nodded.

"Let's see if we can't find somewhere to sit down."

"Sure."

He followed the trooper back inside the building through the empty lobby. He decided not to say anything about what he saw. At least for now.

Thirty-One

Marie dozed on the couch, her knitting needles and an armless sweater in her lap. An old pink housecoat covered her worn white nightgown. Her eyes fluttered open as a pair of headlights lit up the curtains. She breathed a sigh of relief at the familiar sound of the Buick rolling up the street and into the driveway.

The mantle clock showed ten minutes after two.

Marie sat up and set aside her knitting.

Keys jangled softly outside the door. He was being quiet on the porch. The door creaked slowly and Walt stepped into the foyer. He looked surprised to see her.

"You shouldn't have waited up," he said.

Marie clutched at her housecoat. He looked a fright. His clothes dirty and torn, a large welt on his forehead. She stood up. "Walt, what happened to you? You've been gone almost five hours."

Walt opened the closet and hung up his jacket. "It hasn't been that long," he said. "Honey, I'm exhausted. We can talk about it in the morning."

He watched her to see if she'd accept that.

Marie gazed at him, studying what appeared to be various battle scars. He didn't look or sound drunk. Not that she could tell anyway.

He turned and walked down the hallway. Marie heard the icebox door open and close and the suck of a beer bottle opening. She followed him into the kitchen.

"Walt, are you okay?"

He frowned at her. "Everything's fine, Marie. Why don't you go on to bed?"

Marie held silent.

Walt rolled his eyes and sighed. "Look, I had to

repossess a car tonight and I ran into a bit of trouble with the deadbeat, but it wasn't anything I couldn't handle."

Marie looked at her husband closely. "Why are you repossessing cars again? What happened to the man you were using?"

"Waddell? He got a job. He's a cop now." He pulled on the bottle, emptying about half of it. "I'll find someone else next time."

Marie looked away.

"I'm going to wash up a bit. Why don't you go on up to bed?"

Marie nodded and started back down the hall. At the end of the hall she halted. "I forgot. Roger Tully called."

Walt nodded his head as if he weren't surprised by the news. He took another pull on the bottle. "Say what he wanted?"

"No. Just asked if you were home."

"What'd you say?"

Marie looked confused. "I said no."

Walt nodded. "That it?"

"Yes, Walt."

Walt turned away. "I'll be right up."

Marie nodded. Halfway up the stairs she decided that she would believe him.

It would be easier that way.

Thirty-Two

"Where exactly did it happen?"

"HH Road. By the old Eggemeyer farm."

The state trooper looked up from the form. His expression was half bored, half weary. "Where's that?"

"Where you turn onto Lost Creek Road heading north."

The trooper nodded. "And the victim was DOA?"

"That's right."

The trooper scratched something on the form.

They sat at a long table in a corner of the hospital cafeteria. The place was empty and mostly dark, but alive with the soft hum of various stainless steel machines. The trooper was almost young enough to be his son.

"Dead on impact?"

"Alive. Just barely though."

The trooper wrote this down.

"Say anything?"

"One thing. He said, 'I didn't do anything.'"

The trooper looked up. "I didn't do anything?"

"Uh huh."

"Any idea what he meant by that?"

Roger shrugged. "That's what I'd like to know."

The trooper looked at Roger, then he said, "Did you have anything to drink tonight?"

"Just coffee."

The trooper nodded. "So Gideon PD found the kid's car out on Route 3. Any idea what he was doing walking along HH that time of night? That's like six miles from his vehicle."

"Wish I knew," Roger said. "I'm not so sure he was walking along the road. Seemed to me he came out of the

239

woods."

The trooper cocked an eyebrow at Roger. "Out of the woods? You're sure about that?"

"I'm not sure about anything. But it sure seemed that way to me. I thought it was a damned deer at first."

The trooper shook his head and scratched some more on the form. "You say you were coming back from a fishing trip?"

"That's right."

"Rend Lake?"

"Yup."

"Any luck?"

"Huh?"

"Catch anything?"

Roger leaned back in the chair and stretched a cramp out of his leg. "I did all right."

The trooper nodded, then looked down at the form. "How fast were you going?"

Roger shrugged. "About the speed limit, I'd say. Around that."

The trooper wrote that down. "Truck all right?"

"I ain't worried about the truck."

The trooper nodded and lifted his eyes. "Anything to add?"

"Can't think of anything."

The trooper pushed the form over to Roger and handed him his pen.

"Read and sign at the bottom."

Roger looked over the form briefly, signed, and returned the pen to the trooper.

"Hell of a thing," Roger said.

The trooper didn't say anything.

"What about charges?"

"No charges."

The trooper clicked the pen shut and slid it into his

shirt pocket and slipped the form into a folder. He put the folder under his arm and stood up. "You want to notify next of kin or you want me to?"

Roger considered that. "I was thinking I should. The kid's got a grandmother he lives with. Lived with. She might know where to find his mother."

"Okay then. Take it easy, Mr. Tully."

The trooper put out his hand and Roger shook.

"Sorry this happened," the trooper said.

"You and me both."

Thirty-Three

Walt stood at his office window staring across the used car lot. Harvey, his foot resting on a fender of a pickup, was talking to Jimmy Harper, the high school boy who washed cars after school. Sadly, the boy wasn't working out. Walt turned away from the window and sat down at his desk. He stared at the phone a moment before picking it up and dialing Duggan.

He was just about to hang up when Duggan answered.

"We need to talk," said Walt.

"We do?"

"It's about the kid. Ronny Taylor."

"What about him? You talk to him?"

"Well the thing is..."

Walt paused.

"The thing is what?"

"The thing is he's dead."

There was a silence on the other end of the line.

"Say again?"

"It was an accident."

"What do you mean accident?"

"A car accident. You see this truck—"

"Hang on a minute. I can't hear you."

Walt waited. A long moment passed.

Duggan came back on the line. "Goddamn toilet. Okay. Tell me again. What happened?"

"It wasn't me. I don't even have a truck—"

"Walt, quit jerking me around. Now what happened?"

"I told you. He got hit by a truck."

"The Taylor kid?"

"Yes!"

"And he's dead?"

"Uh huh."

"Jesus," Duggan said. "When did this happen?"

"Last night."

"Christ. So do we know who hit him?"

"Roger Tully hit him."

"Who the fuck's Roger Tully?"

"The coroner."

Duggan fumed. "Walt, you ain't making any sense. Are you telling me the coroner killed the Taylor kid?"

"It was an accident."

"An accident?"

Walt stood up. He paced nervously about the room. He looked out the window. The Harper kid was sponging off a Chevy. Harvey was gone. "Pretty much."

"Pretty much," Duggan said. "Walt, where the fuck were you when this happened?"

Walt made no reply.

"Walt?"

"I was...there."

"You were there? In the car?"

"No, no. In the woods."

"Oh for fuck's sake. Walt I don't know what the fuck you're talking about here."

"He was about to confess. He was about to tell me—"

"Walt, just tell me what the fuck happened."

Walt turned and stumbled into a golf bag. The bag slid along the wall and crashed to the floor. Walt stepped over it. "I drove him out past Lost Creek Road. Out in the sticks. To put the fear of God him, like you said."

"Whoa, like I said?"

"You said—"

"I didn't say kill the sonofabitch!"

"I told you, Roger hit him."

"The coroner."

"Yeah. You said put the fear of God in him, so I did.

And it was working. He was talking, he was about to tell me what happened."

"I don't understand. You drove him out there?"

"I drove him."

"You fucking kidnapped him?"

"No, no..."

"But you had a gun?"

"How was I supposed to put the fear of God in him without a gun?"

"So how..."

"It wasn't loaded."

"Never mind. I don't want to know. Walt, kidnapping is a federal fucking offense!"

"Who said anything about kidnapping? He got a flat. So I gave him a ride."

"Walt. I don't understand a word you're saying."

"I—"

"You know the coroner?"

"Of course. We're good friends."

"Fucking Christ! Walt, this don't sound like no accident here."

"Look, I'm trying to tell you. The kid ran out into the highway and Roger hit him."

"Okay, I'm counting like four major felonies here. Jeez. Look, do me a fucking favor and pretend you never talked to me. Okay? You don't know me from Adam, okay? Christ."

"It was an accident. I told you. Roger never even saw him."

"There ain't no fucking accidents, Walt. Somebody dies fleeing a kidnapping, it's the same as murder."

Walt turned pale and his mouth dried up.

"Does anyone else know about this? What about the coroner, what does he know?"

"I don't know."

"You don't know? You don't fucking know?"

"I'm not sure."

"But he might?"

"I don't know!" Walt cried.

"No, of course not. Christ. This coroner, he better be a good fucking friend, Walt, otherwise you're going away a long fucking time. Jesus, Mary and Joseph."

"It was dark."

"It was dark," Duggan repeated. "Listen Walt, do me a favor, okay? Don't call me again. Okay? As in never. Can you do that?"

"I—"

The line went dead.

Walt set down the phone. With a trembling hand he pulled a cigarette from the pack on the desk. Between drags he sat listening to his heart thud. The kid had been about to talk. He was certain. Another minute and he would've had the truth. If only Roger hadn't...

Christ, what was he doing talking to Duggan anyway? A greasy sonofabitch like that, he'd just as soon blackmail him as give him the time of day. Give me five grand or I go to the cops. Ten grand. Christ. Why hadn't he kept his big mouth shut?

Duggan was right though. He'd killed the kid, just as surely as if he'd pulled a trigger. And he'd pay for it. One way or another.

He stubbed out the cigarette in the ashtray as someone rapped on the door. Walt started and looked up.

Harvey poked his head in the room. "Stepping out for lunch, okay Buddy?"

"Sure."

"Oh and Roger Tully's here."

"Roger?"

"Uh huh. I'll tell him you're off the phone."

Walt looked around his desk absently. "Yeah. Thanks."

246

For Christ's sake.

Roger stood in the doorway wearing his unofficial coroner's uniform, a canvas fishing jacket and a fly-fishing hat covered with dozens of hand-tied flies and a black and white coroner button. He wasn't smiling.

Walt stood up behind the desk. "Roger, Jesus, I heard about the accident."

Roger nodded silently, his mouth set rigid in a blank face. He stepped into the office.

"I've been meaning to come by."

"Were you now?"

Walt swallowed hard. "Pull up a seat," he said, motioning toward a chair. "How you doing? You doing all right?"

Roger held silent.

"So what brings you in?"

Roger slouched in the chair, his hands folded in his pockets. He let out a long sigh. "This ain't easy, Walt. Us being friends and all."

Walt fiddled nervously with a pencil. "What is it, Rog?"

"I think you know."

Walt shook his head and frowned at him. "What do I know, Rog? What are you trying to say?"

"The other night, out on HH Road—"

"Where you had your accident?"

"Yeah. *My* accident."

Roger paused. "Walt, what do you suppose that Taylor kid was doing out there in the middle of nowhere, that time of night?"

Walt shrugged. "A shitbird like that. Who knows?"

"Uh huh. And you don't know nothing about it?"

Walt laughed dryly. "Why would I?"

"Yeah. Why would you?"

They fell silent a moment.

Walt frowned irritably. "Okay Rog. If you got something to say, why don't you come out with it? Enough of this pussyfooting around."

Roger nodded. "I seen you, buddy. I seen you out there the other night. On HH Road, in the trees. I seen the service revolver in your hand."

Walt breathed in steadily and looked down at his desk. He picked up the pack of Lucky Strikes and removed a cigarette from the pack, then offered the pack to Roger.

Roger shook his head.

Walt picked up the Zippo from his desk and lit the cigarette and tossed the lighter back on the desk. He sent a jet of smoke toward the ceiling. For some reason he seemed remarkably calm.

"I don't know what you think you saw, Rog, but I know what you didn't see. You didn't see me. That I guaran-damn-tee."

"I called your home around one o'clock. Marie was still up. She said you weren't home."

"That's right. I was repossessing a vehicle."

Roger stared flatly across the desk.

Walt said, "We're having a hell of time finding people willing to work."

Roger leaned forward and lowered his voice slightly. "Look buddy, let's cut the crap. You were out there with Ronny Taylor. You probably dragged him out there to scare him into confessing to killing Emily. That's why you carried the revolver. Only he got away from you. And that's where I came in. He tried to flag down my truck only I never saw him."

"But you think you saw me."

Roger nodded. "It was you. No mistake about that."

Walt tapped his ash on the rim of a cigarette tray. "And I guess it won't do no good to have you talk to the deadbeat whose car I repossessed?"

"Someone whose car you repossessed is going to be your alibi?"

Walt shrugged and looked away. Then he turned back to Roger. "Why are you here, Roger?"

"I think you know why."

"Tell me anyway."

"Look Walt, I haven't mentioned this to anyone. I've kept it to myself even though that was wrong. I wanted to give you a chance to come forward on your own." Roger waved a drifting cloud of smoke from in front of his face. "But I'm done waiting. Buddy, you need to turn yourself in."

"Come on, Rog—"

"I'm serious."

Walt grinned nervously. "Or?"

"Or I will."

He would too. Walt knew Roger well enough to know when he was serious. He knew it was pointless to try to talk him out of it. The bastard wouldn't lie to save his own skin. Never had, never would.

Walt set the cigarette in the ashtray, his hand trembling slightly. He leaned forward, his elbows on the desk, hands folded beneath his chin. "Okay, Rog, let's say you're right. Let's say, for the sake of argument, I don't have an alibi. Do you have any idea what we're talking about here? Kidnapping. Manslaughter. Assault with a deadly weapon. Maybe even second-degree murder."

Roger stared silently.

"They could send me away for the rest of my goddamn life."

"Walt, they're going to find out eventually. Trust me, it'll go easier on you if you turn yourself in."

Walt scoffed. "They couldn't find their ass with both hands and a road map! You know that! They couldn't find out a damn thing about my daughter."

249

Roger sat up. "It's the right thing to do, Walt."

"Bullshit! Leaving my wife and son without a father is the right thing?" He lowered his voice again, his tone softening. "Roger, this will destroy them."

"It's the only way."

Walt stared hard at Roger. "Goddamn it, Roger, we're best friends!"

"If you want to remain friends you'll do what's right."

Walt slowly shook his head. He turned and stared through the window and watched as a black Plymouth drove onto the lot. It looked like Doc Toenjes' Plymouth. And Harvey was gone. Walt turned back to Roger, choking on his words. "He was going to talk. He was going to tell me..."

"Who?"

"The kid. Taylor."

"Walt, he was scared. He would have told you anything."

"You're wrong. He knew. Goddamn it, I'm telling you he knew."

Walt stared down at his hands a moment, his eyes scalding. The room seemed to be closing in on him, and he struggled for breath. He shook himself and slowly stood up. He stepped out from behind the desk, his footsteps heavy, like he was walking in cement.

"Of course, you're right, Roger. You always are."

Roger lowered his eyes, unable to meet his friend's gaze. "I'm going to do everything I can for you and—"

He turned to look at Walt.

The club made a short whooshing sound, then a dull flat crack as the head connected with the base of Roger's skull. The shaft snapped in half and the club's head sailed across the room shattering a framed photograph. The picture crashed to the floor.

Roger let out a short, breathless cry. He spilled out of

the chair onto his hands and knees. His hands shot up to the long deep gash at the base of his skull.

Walt gazed absently at the broken shaft in his hand, then he looked down at Roger doubled over on the floor. He raised the club and began hammering Roger's head with the splintered shaft.

"He...knew! He...knew!" he cried between blows.

Roger crawled blindly after Walt, attempting to latch onto his legs. He caught hold of one of his knees, but Walt shook him off and swatted him in the face with the club. Roger lunged, wrapping his arms around both legs. He held on fiercely, like he was trying to bring down a runningback.

Walt's eyes flashed and he grasped the shaft of the club with both hands. He raised it above his head and with a low, base growl plunged the jagged edge between Roger's shoulder blades. The crunch and snap of wood on bone echoed throughout the little office.

Roger collapsed with a heavy groan. He laid still, his breath shallow and ragged.

Walt stood over his friend, trembling, his chest heaving, sweat rolling off his face in rivulets.

He stepped backward and sat on the edge of the desk, breathing heavily. "You don't understand, Rog," he said in short gasps. "I have a family. I have responsibilities."

Roger was silent, still.

"Hello?" A male voice echoed down the corridor from the showroom. Walt gazed toward the door, then back to Roger where he lay in a heap on the linoleum floor. The room commenced spinning and he felt his breakfast coming up. He dove for a wastebasket.

When he finished vomiting he sat on the floor beside the wastebasket, and wiped the bile on his sleeve.

"Anybody here?"

Footsteps sounded in the hallway. Walt crawled to his

feet and went over to the door and quietly turned the lock. Then he leaned against the door and waited for the spinning to pass. He studied Roger, sprawled spread eagle on the floor, the shaft of the club protruding from his back like a jig doll, a spreading pool of blood like melted red licorice.

Walt gazed blearily around the room and eyes fell on the closet. He got to his feet and opened the closet door and peered inside. The closet was a mere four feet deep and crammed with cardboard boxes: old fliers, balloons, giveaways and other useless crap. He hefted a half dozen boxes and piled them beside a filing cabinet, pausing between each box to catch his breath and wipe the sweat from his brow. Then he turned back to Roger. Stooping, he seized him by the wrists and dragged him across the floor. He muscled him into the closet and shut the door.

The door bounced off one of Roger's ankles, but he gave no sign that he felt anything.

Walt squatted and folded up one of his legs.

He happened to glance up and caught Roger's glassy stare. Blood trickled from his mouth and nose. Roger made to speak and a bubble of blood foamed on his lips. The bubble burst and he wheezed weakly.

Walt stood up and wedged his shoulder against the door till he heard the latch click.

Then he picked up the broken club and cracked picture frame and tossed them in the metal drawer of the filing cabinet behind a row of folders.

He scanned the room. Roger's fly-fishing hat lay in the small pool of blood that gelled on the floor. From it stretched a long crimson trail that ended at the closet door.

"Hello?"

Walt muttered a curse and scooped up Roger's hat and quietly opened the cabinet drawer and dropped it inside.

Then he checked himself and his clothes. Blood spattered his white shirt and his tie and slacks. It was on his hands too. And his shoes. Goddamn blood was everywhere.

Beneath the door a shadow appeared. Someone knocked sharply.

Walt stood in the center of the room, motionless, holding his breath.

From the closet came a low, soft moan.

Leather shoes squeaked just outside the door. "Any one here?"

Walt grit his teeth. He gazed toward the window wondering how long it would take him to clamber through.

Too long.

The man stood outside the door a moment, then muttered something under his breath, then his footsteps receded down the hallway.

Walt went to the window and watched as a man in a gray suit exited the showroom and climbed into the black Plymouth and drove off the lot. It was the dentist, all right.

He let go a sigh of relief and unlocked the office door and hurried down the hallway to the broom closet for the mop and bucket.

When the office was clean, Walt scribbled "out to lunch" on the back of an old flyer and taped it to the showroom door and walked out to the Buick. Roger's old International sat in front of the dealership like a big yellow flag. He gazed at the old truck, unable to decide what to do about it. He felt utterly exhausted, completely drained, like he had no thoughts left.

He looked at the truck again, then climbed into the Buick and drove home.

Thirty-Four

He caught a break. Marie was out back picking herbs from the garden. He slipped inside and found a brown paper bag under the kitchen sink. He climbed upstairs to the linen closet and stuffed a random bed sheet into the bag. Then he opened the bedroom closet and selected a clean shirt and tie and a pair of gray slacks similar to the ones he had on and stepped into the bathroom and locked the door. He got undressed and slipped into the clean shirt and slacks and knotted the tie, then he used his blood-spattered shirt to wipe his shoes. He stuffed the bloody shirt and pants into the bag and checked himself in the mirror and opened the door.

Marie stood there.

"I heard you pull up," she said. "I didn't know you were coming home for lunch. I would have made—"

Walt stepped around her. "Can't stay for lunch. Just need to grab a few things and get back."

Marie studied the paper bag. "Well, there's some tuna salad in the fridge..."

Walt stopped and turned and gave Marie a quick peck on the forehead. "Got to go. Love you."

She followed him downstairs and watched him leave through the front door. She called out, "I'm making pot roast for dinner."

The screen door slammed behind him.

Back at the dealership he found Harvey talking to the man with a black Plymouth, showing him one of the new Ford Fairlanes.

"Oh, Walt!" Harvey said.

"Walt waved, smiled and kept walking.

"Can you step over—?"

"Be with you in a minute," said Walt. He stepped inside the showroom and walked down the hall to his office, locking the door behind him.

He went to the closet and put his ear against the door.

Silence.

He slowly opened the door. Roger tilted to one side, his eyes thin red slits, mouth hanging loosely.

Walt squatted, trying to determine whether he was dead or alive.

A strange sound, half moan, half rattle, came from deep inside his throat.

The sonofabitch was still alive.

"For Christ's sake. Why don't you die?" Walt hissed.

He removed the bloody white shirt from the paper bag and fashioned a gag, wrapping the sleeves twice around Roger's blood-sticky head before tying a knot.

Roger's eyes blinked slowly, then closed.

Walt stood up and tossed the paper bag inside the closet.

"You think I planned this?" he said in a loud whisper. "You think I wanted this? All I wanted was to know what happened to my little girl. All you had to do was look the other way." Walt's voice caught in the back of his throat and his eyes stung. "Goddamn it, Rog, you were my best friend."

He swallowed the lump in his throat and slammed the door.

Thirty-Five

Walt slumped red-eyed and sore at his desk, burning through cigarette after cigarette, till he'd gone through most of the emergency pack he stowed in the bottom drawer. He'd told Harvey he needed to catch up on paperwork.

There was no paperwork. Instead he stared at the closet door, ears pricked for anything, but heard only the whir of passing motorcars, the flapping of strings of colored pennants in the breeze, Harvey hacking up a lung out in the showroom, or simply his overactive imagination. He was reminded of the Poe story he'd been forced to read in grade school where the murderer believes he hears the corpse's heart beating beneath the floorboards. Eventually the sound drives him mad and he confesses everything to the cops.

It was a good thing there weren't any cops around.

Twice — first around two o'clock and again at half past three — his conscience began to get the better of him and he almost picked up the phone and called for an ambulance. Both times he set the phone back into its cradle before dialing the operator. What the hell good would an ambulance do if Roger were dead already?

He *was* dead, wasn't he?

Walt stood up and went over to the closet and pressed his ear against the smooth wood of the door.

Again, silence.

He went back to his desk and sat down and chewed his fingernails till they were raw and bloody then he laid his head on his arms on his desk and tried to rest. When he looked up again, after what seemed hours, it was four o'clock.

He ran his fingers through his hair and fought the urge to tear his hair out. Or scream. Something.

"Hold it together, goddamn it," he whispered.

On Mondays, Harvey went home at five thirty. Early enough to eat dinner before the town council meeting. If he could just hang on till then. Then he'd go home for dinner, get some rest, and come back around ten or so, after the town rolled up the sidewalks.

Then what?

He had a few vague ideas.

He recalled something he'd read once, something about a murder, back before the war, and how this guy's body had been dumped and later found in one of the strip mine ponds over in Bond County. The dead man was a labor organizer. There were dozens, if not hundreds of strip mine ponds dotting Greene County. Some had been stocked with blue gill and crappie, others were swimming with toxic metals and shit like that. These were marked with signs. No Swimming. No Fishing. No Trespassing. Walt figured he could fill Roger's pockets with stones and let him sink silently into the toxic sludge. Maybe it would even dissolve the bones and teeth and leave no trace. No body, no murder. If he could just figure a way in. Most of those ponds were fenced off with tall hurricane fences and razor wire. What he wouldn't give for a pair of bolt cutters. Buying a pair now would be a bad idea.

As a last resort, he might bury him somewhere. Out on Lost Creek where he'd taken the Taylor boy. Spend half the night digging a grave.

Who the hell was he kidding? He'd never get away with it. A guy like Roger Tully, the county coroner, he goes missing, that's news. There'd be investigations. The state might even get involved. He'd be better off going down to the station right now, turning himself in.

There was a loud rapping on the door. Walt felt his

heart almost leap through his chest.

"Hey Walt?"

"Yeah Harv?"

Harvey tried to open the door, but found it locked. Walt got up and unlocked the door.

"Hey Walt, sorry to bother you. I need to run over to the bank a minute."

"Sure."

"Be back in fifteen minutes."

"Okay. Anybody out there?"

"Might as well be a mortuary."

Walt laughed faintly.

"Oh, and I noticed Roger Tully's truck's still out there."

"Yeah."

"Banged up pretty good, ain't it?"

"Uh huh."

Walt's eyes shifted toward the closet, then back to Harvey.

"We doing something with it?"

"Yeah. I'll take care of it."

"How's he doing?"

"Who?"

"Roger. He looked a little shaken up."

"Oh. He's all right. You know Roger."

Harvey nodded. He started to close the door and stopped. "You want this door closed?"

"You can leave it open."

Walt waited till he heard Harvey exit the building then he walked through the showroom and out the front doors where Roger had left the pickup. The windshield was splintered and Roger had duct-taped one of the headlights in place. Walt looked in the driver's side window. The keys hung from the ignition switch. The cab smelled awful, like rotten fish. It was crammed with tackle boxes, fishing poles, a dirty Styrofoam cooler, probably full of rancid catfish, and up in the rear window a gun rack holding Roger's old goose gun.

What the hell was he going to do with this piece of junk?

Walt sagged against the truck's door. It was all too much. All of it. When they came looking for Roger they'd know exactly where he was last seen. Walt's office.

He opened the door and eased into the pickup. The engine turned right over. He backed up the truck and pulled around to the back of the building and parked it next to a few rundown trade-ins.

He sat in the cab too drained to think or even move. He was just so goddamn tired. He tried to tell himself that everything he'd done he'd done for his family. That no matter what happened, they were all that mattered. For them he'd figure something out. For them he'd keep going, no matter how bad or hopeless things looked.

Once he got some rest.

Thirty-Six

After dinner Walt and Jimmy went into the living room to listen to the ball game. Jimmy lay on the sofa and Gary the cat curled up on his chest. He stroked the cat between the ears and he purred happily. Walt lounged in the easy chair and closed his eyes, but his nerves were too frayed to nap. Marie put away the dishes then carried her sewing basket into the room.

In the bottom of the eighth Walt stood up and stretched. "Going out for a bit."

Marie looked up from her mending. "Oh Walt, honey you promised."

"Now Marie. Won't take more than an hour."

"But it's almost ten o'clock."

Walt scowled at her. "I know what time it is."

He went to the hallway closet and slipped on his gray jacket.

Marie was beside him. She spoke softly, trying not to rile him. "Walt, what's going on?"

Walt zipped up the jacket. He took Marie by the arms and tried to smile reassuringly. "This is the last time. I promise."

"The last time for what?"

"The last time I'm going out at night. Promise."

"Is it another repossession?"

"Marie, it's nothing to concern yourself about. I'll be home in an hour or two."

He went out the door and turned and walked around the house to the shed, trying not to draw any attention to himself. There was no light in the shed and he knocked around for a while trying to find his wire cutters. He fished around in his pockets for his Zippo, but it wasn't there. He wedged open the door with a garden hoe to let in the moonlight, but he still couldn't see a damn thing.

He stepped back and knocked over a rake, setting off a series of garden implement collisions. A neighbor's dog barked.

The porch light came on.

Walt kicked the door closed.

"Walt?"

He remained still.

He waited in the shed till the light went out. Hell with this, he thought. I'll get some tools from the garage.

Moments later he pulled up behind the car dealership. He eased out of the Buick and popped the trunk, then he unlocked the back door and slipped inside. He walked down the hallway to his office and unlocked the door.

He stepped inside his office and closed the door. He kept the light off and waited a moment for his eyes to adjust. Then he felt his way over to the closet and pressed his ear against the wood.

There was no sound.

He took a deep breath and opened the closet door.

Too dark to see. He reached up pulled the chain on the overhead bulb.

Roger was gone.

The bloodstained shirt lay bunched on the floor next to the broken club. The brown paper bag lay crumpled in the corner.

Walt spun around, his heart in his throat. His eyes darted about the room. He crept across the floor to his desk and guardedly looked behind it.

Nothing.

He peered out the window into the lot, not quite sure what he expected to see there. The night was quiet.

In the window behind the desk he caught a brief movement. He turned and found himself facing Roger, a

12-gauge shotgun cradled in his arms.

Roger's voice wheezed. "Looking for something, Walt?"

Walt swallowed. "Shit, Rog, you almost gave me a heart attack."

Roger sagged against the doorframe, the barrel trained on Walt. He was pale and trembled at the effort of standing upright.

"Real sorry about that." Roger coughed and winced at the pain. "I didn't mean..."

Walt shoved his hands in his pockets. "Roger, you're hurt. You got to let me get you some help."

"Very sweet. Very thoughtful," said Roger, his voice scarcely rising above a whisper. "Sit down, Walt."

"Rog, c'mon."

Roger lifted the shotgun.

"Sit!" he cried, his face contorted grotesquely with pain.

Walt sank slowly to his chair.

"Hands on the desk...where I can see them."

"Look Rog, I messed up, okay. I know it. Jesus, don't I know it. I don't know what the hell got into me. I just lost my goddamn head..."

Somewhere across town a siren could be heard. The blood seemed to drain from Walt's face.

Roger said, "I called soon as I saw you drive up."

Walt nodded toward the shotgun. "Your father's goose gun, ain't it?"

"That's right."

"You never could hit a damn thing with it."

"I did all right."

"Well I just might just have to test that—"

"I wouldn't, Walt."

Walt smiled thinly. He stood up and came out from behind the desk, slowly, deliberately. "What the hell, Rog.

It's over for me, anyway. We both know that."

"Walt..."

A wistful look came into his eye. "You know, all I ever wanted was to look after my family. Why couldn't I? How is it, Rog? I failed Emily. I failed them all."

"Stop, Walt."

"Do me a favor, Rog. In the chest, Okay?"

"Stay back now, Walt," Roger said. "Damn it, I mean it."

"The chest, Rog."

Roger swallowed hard.

Walt came on, his eyes on locked on Roger's.

Roger lowered the gun till the barrel was aimed at Walt's thigh. "You bastard, don't make me do it."

Walt took hold of the barrel and raised it to his chest.

"That's it. Go on now."

Roger stared hard at Walt and his eyes narrowed to folded slits.

Walt jerked the shotgun away and in one quick motion placed the barrel against Roger's chest and pulled the trigger.

There was a dull click.

Walt stared at him blankly.

Roger shrugged. "Guess I forgot to load it."

Out front a patrol car screamed onto the lot, lights flashing through the window and spinning off the walls. The cruiser skidded to a stop outside the showroom doors, sending a cloud of white dust drifting over the lot.

Walt looked at Roger and grinned. "You wouldn't happen to have a shell I can borrow, old buddy?"

Roger shook his head.

Walt tossed Roger the shotgun and turned around and walked back to his desk. He dropped into the chair and with a trembling hand took the last cigarette from the pack on his desk. He flicked open the lighter and lit the cigarette and leaned forward, his elbows on his desk, and ran a hand through his hair.

He could hear the cops rattling the locked front doors.

"I guess I'll never know what happened to her," he said.

They could hear the cops passing outside the window on their way to the rear of the building.

Roger leaned the shotgun against the wall and scuffled across the room and eased carefully into the chair across from Walt's desk, his eyes damp from pain. "She died, Walt. That's what happened to her. People we love die. Knowing why won't bring her back."

Roger winced and tried to sit in a way that it didn't hurt so much, but if there was one he couldn't find it. "It hurts the same...knowing or not knowing."

Walt looked at Roger. "I'm such a goddamn fool. Rog, will you ever forgive me?"

The cops found the open back door. There were rapid footfalls in the hallway.

"I already have," Roger said.

The cops entered the office, weapons drawn.

Walt chuckled and looked at the cops. "A goddamn saint," Walt said. "If I've said it once, I've said it a hundred times. A goddamn saint."

Thirty-Seven

Fred Eggemeyer lounged on the bench outside the barbershop, a newspaper folded on his lap. The morning sun had just cleared the rooftops and now flooded the street. The warmth pored over him and seemed to daze him, like a swamp turtle on a rock. Fred glanced up as Bob Jennings stepped outside and untied his apron and sat beside him on the bench.

"Shaping up to be a nice day."

"Yep."

"That this week's paper?"

"Uh huh." Fred handed over the *Herald-Tribune*.

Bob shoved the paper under his arm and removed his bulldog pipe from the pocket of his barber coat. He thumbed the bowl full of Captain Black and struck a match on the brick wall and puffed on the pipe till it was going good and strong. He waved the match out and tossed it away.

"Been up to see Roger Tully?" he said.

"Last night."

"How's he doing?"

"Not too bad. Ready to get out and do some fishing. They say he'll be in for another week."

Bob puffed thoughtfully on his pipe. "What was it he had, a punctured lung?"

"And two broke ribs."

"That's got to hurt."

"They got him on some stuff so he don't feel it too bad. Morphine, I believe."

Nothing was said for a few minutes. Then Bob said, "Paper say what they charged Walt Ahrens with?"

Fred folded his arms over his belly. "One charge of

second-degree murder... One charge attempted murder ...
Assault and battery."

"Yeah."

"Feds could charge him with kidnapping too, what I
hear."

Bob nodded and shook open the newspaper.

Fred stared off down the street toward the bank where
the mail truck idled noisily. The mailman was nowhere in
sight.

The barber took the pipe from his mouth. "Never
would've believed it."

Fred grunted in agreement.

"Goes to show you just never know people."

"Uh huh."

They fell silent. Fred watched a shiny new tractor roll
past.

"Saw the drugstore's for sale," he said.

"Saw the sign driving in this morning."

"Reckon Miller'll be moving back to St. Louis. Ain't
that where he's from?"

"Somewhere round there. Clayton, I believe it was."

"Too bad. Town needs a drugstore."

"Yeah it does."

"I never had a problem with him."

"You mean him being Jewish?"

"Uh huh."

"Course not. Why would you?"

"Never thought he had anything to do with that girl's
death."

"Hell no. Course some people did."

"Well, yeah. There's always going to be a few..."

Bob tapped his pipe on the wall. "What do you reckon
did happen to that girl?"

Fred gazed off down the street as the silence ticked by.
At length he said, "I reckon it was just one of those things."

Bob looked at Fred Eggemeyer for a moment, then he nodded. "Yeah."

For a while, they sat still, reading the paper and watching the cars pass. Then Fred stood up with a deep groan and stretched his arms. He looked up the street and yawned. "Think I'll wander over to the newspaper. See if there's any news since the paper come out."

"You mean see if Jenna Hellebusch is there, don't you?"

Fred felt himself blush. Then he shoved his hands deep his bib pockets, and tramped off down the sidewalk.

Thank you for reading.

Please review this book. Reviews help others find New Pulp Press and inspire us to keep providing these marvelous tales.

If you would like to be put on our email list to receive updates on new releases, contests, and promotions, please go to NewPulpPress.com and sign up.

About The Author

Chris Orlet was born and raised in Belleville, Illinois. He has worked a multitude of dead-end jobs, including bartender, sportswriter, gun seller, Peace Corps volunteer, tech writer, salesman for a trailer parts company, and other occupations too unsavory to mention. He lives in Saint Louis, Missouri with his wife, son, and dachshund. This is his first novel.

www.newpulppress.com

www.ingramcontent.com/pod-product-compliance
Lightning Source LLC
Chambersburg PA
CBHW060528260626
47161CB00003B/808